MARVEL DOODLES

Written by
Kurt Hartman and Tomas Palacios

Illustrated by
Tomás Montalvo-Lagos

Printed in the United States of America

First Edition, October 2016

1 3 5 7 9 10 8 6 4 2

ISBN 978-1-4847-8636-9

FAC-008598-16232

Library of Congress Control Number: 2016932821

Designed by Kurt Hartman

Los Angeles
New York

SUSTAINABLE FORESTRY INITIATIVE — Certified Sourcing
www.sfiprogram.org
SFI-00993
This Label Applies to Text Stock Only

Who is hanging out with Spider-Man on the rooftops of New York City? Draw him some friends!

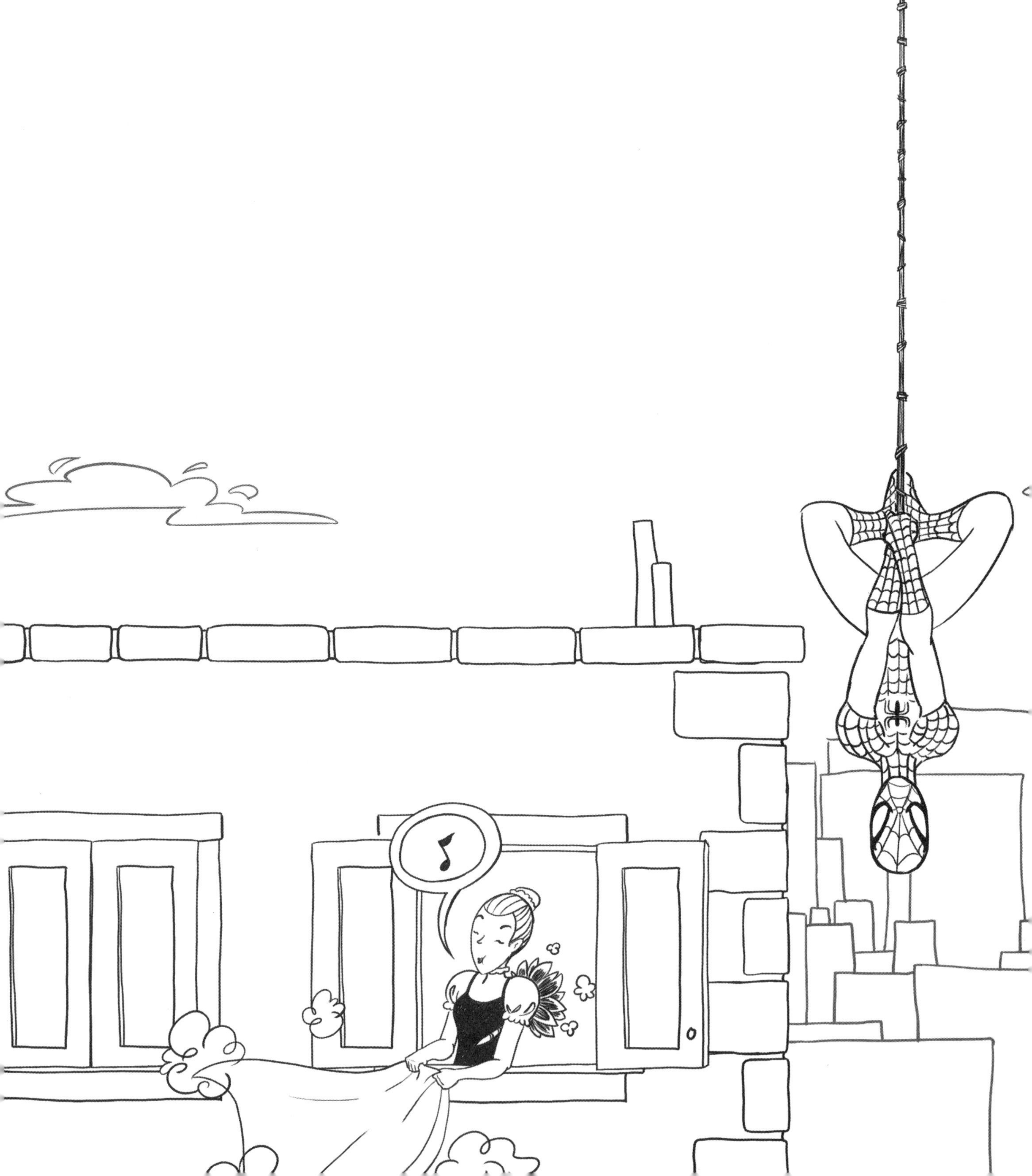

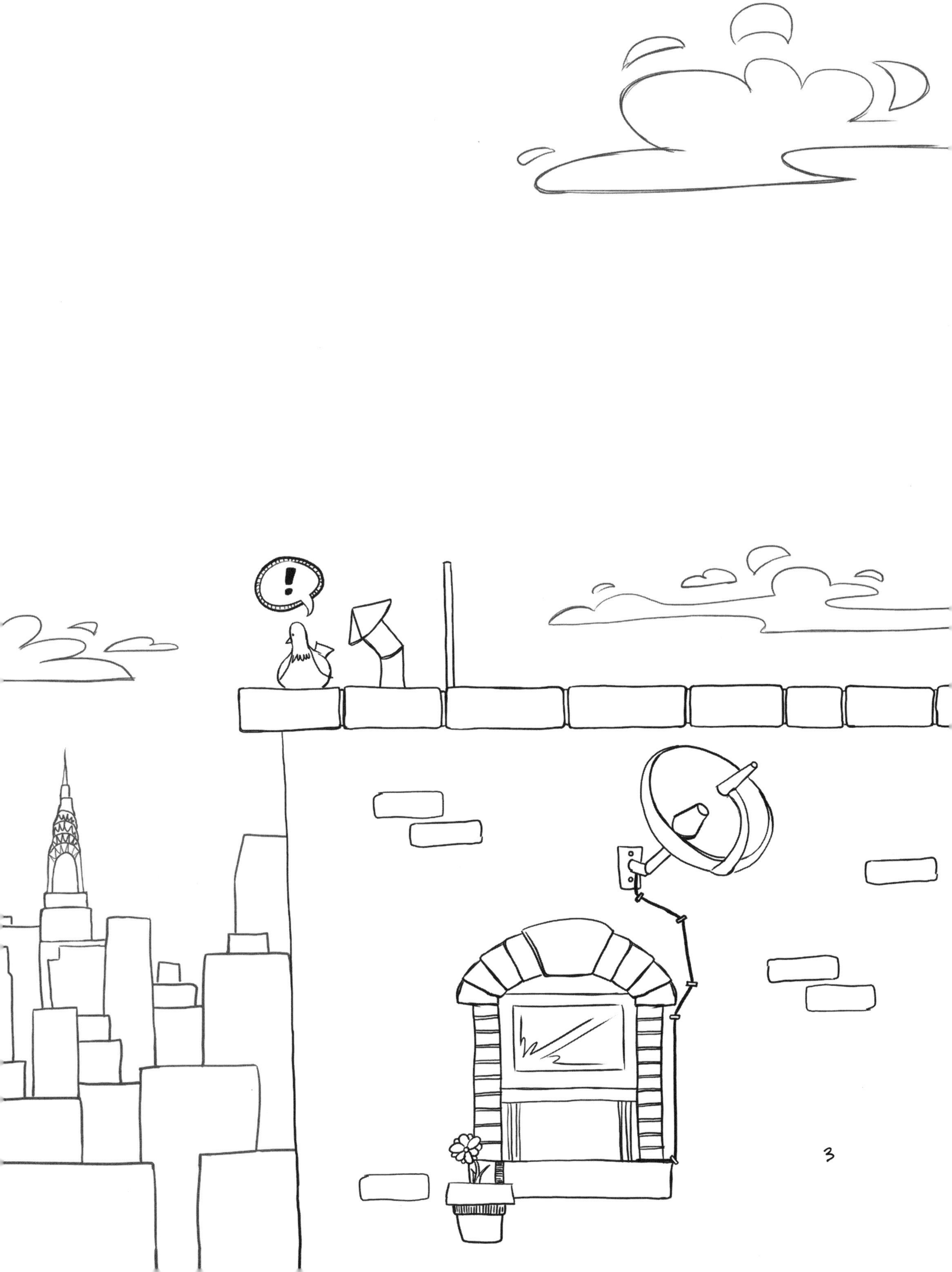
!

Doctor Strange is thinking of some cool magic!
What is he thinking about?

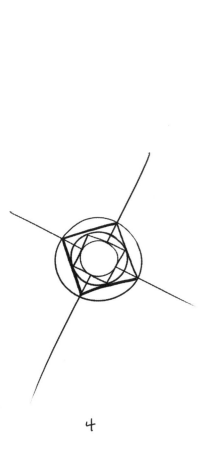

Help Groot hide.
Draw some trees and bushes around him.

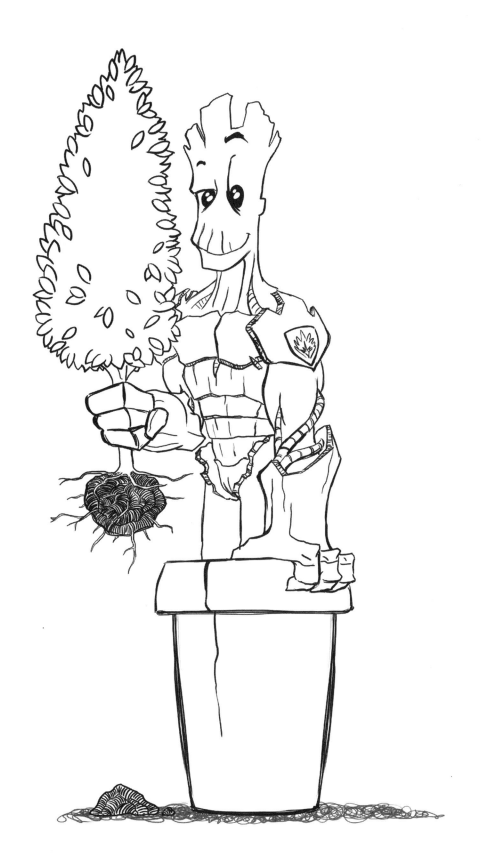

Rocket has built a new invention.
What does it look like?

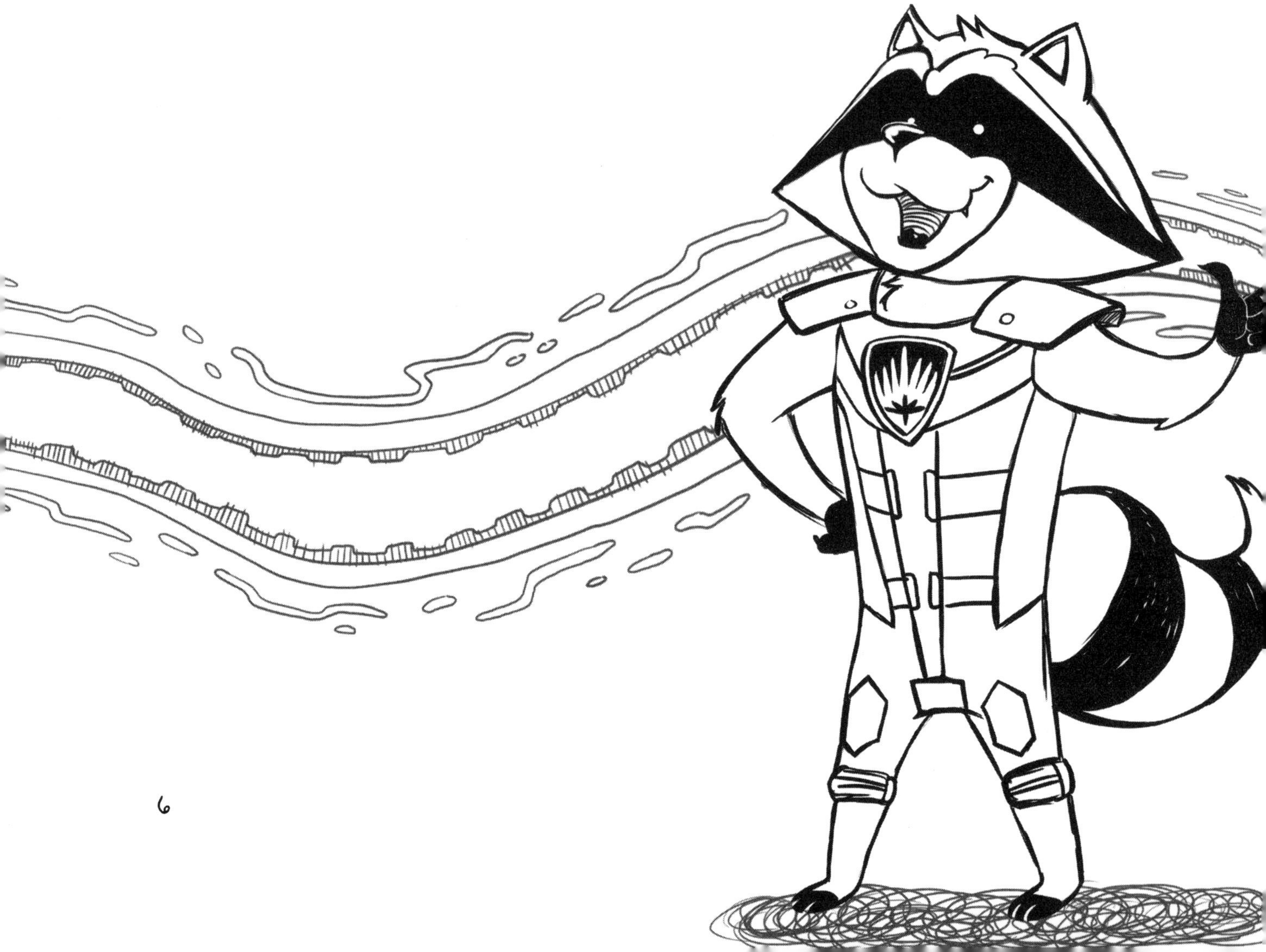

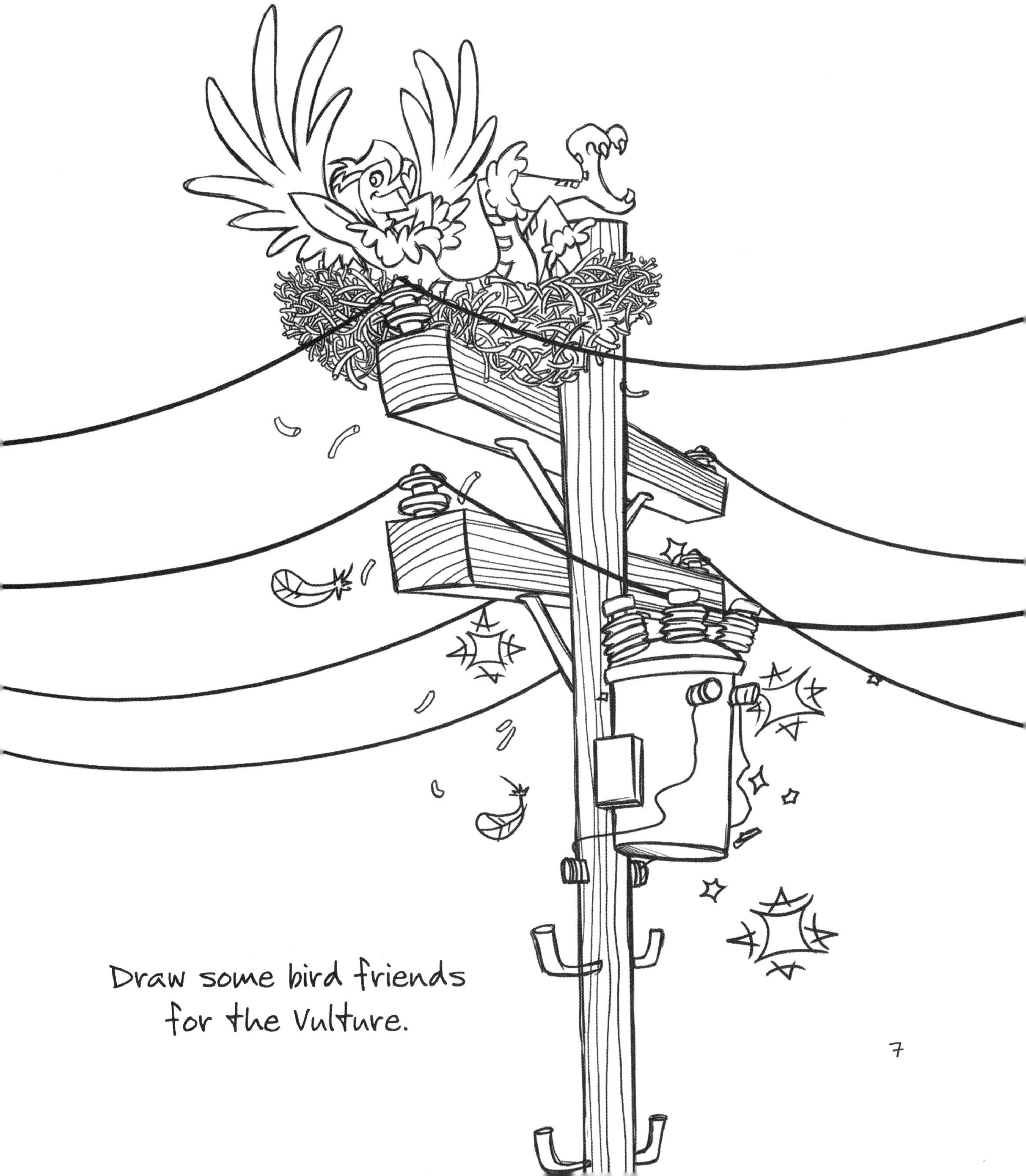

Draw some bird friends
for the Vulture.

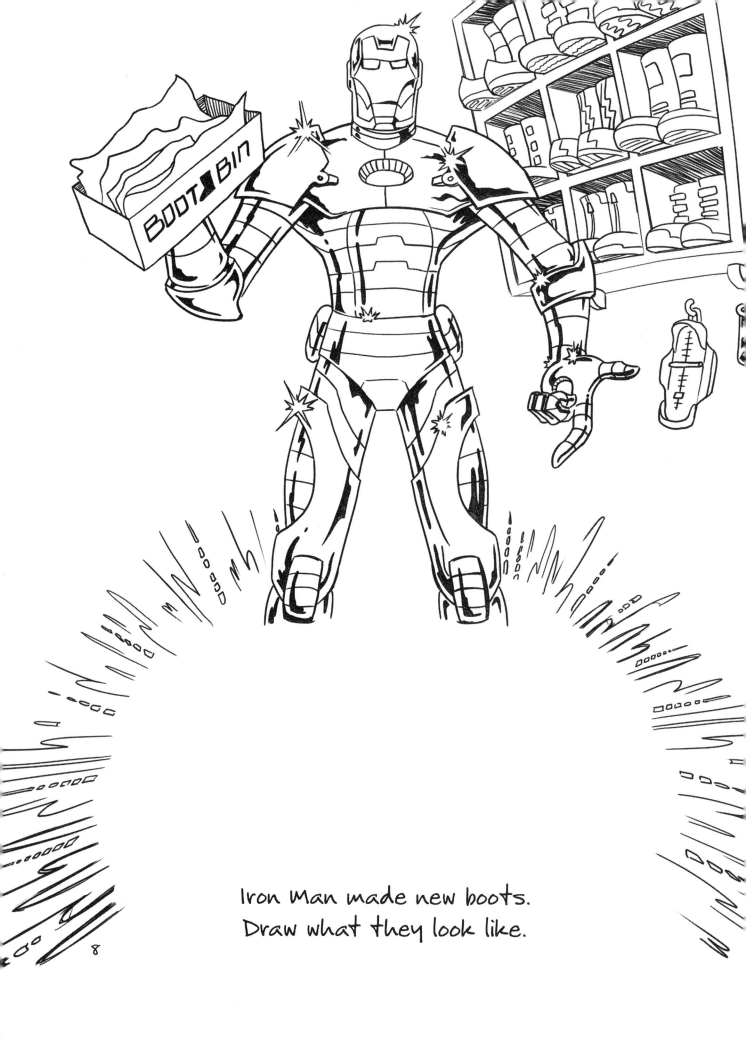

Iron Man made new boots.
Draw what they look like.

8

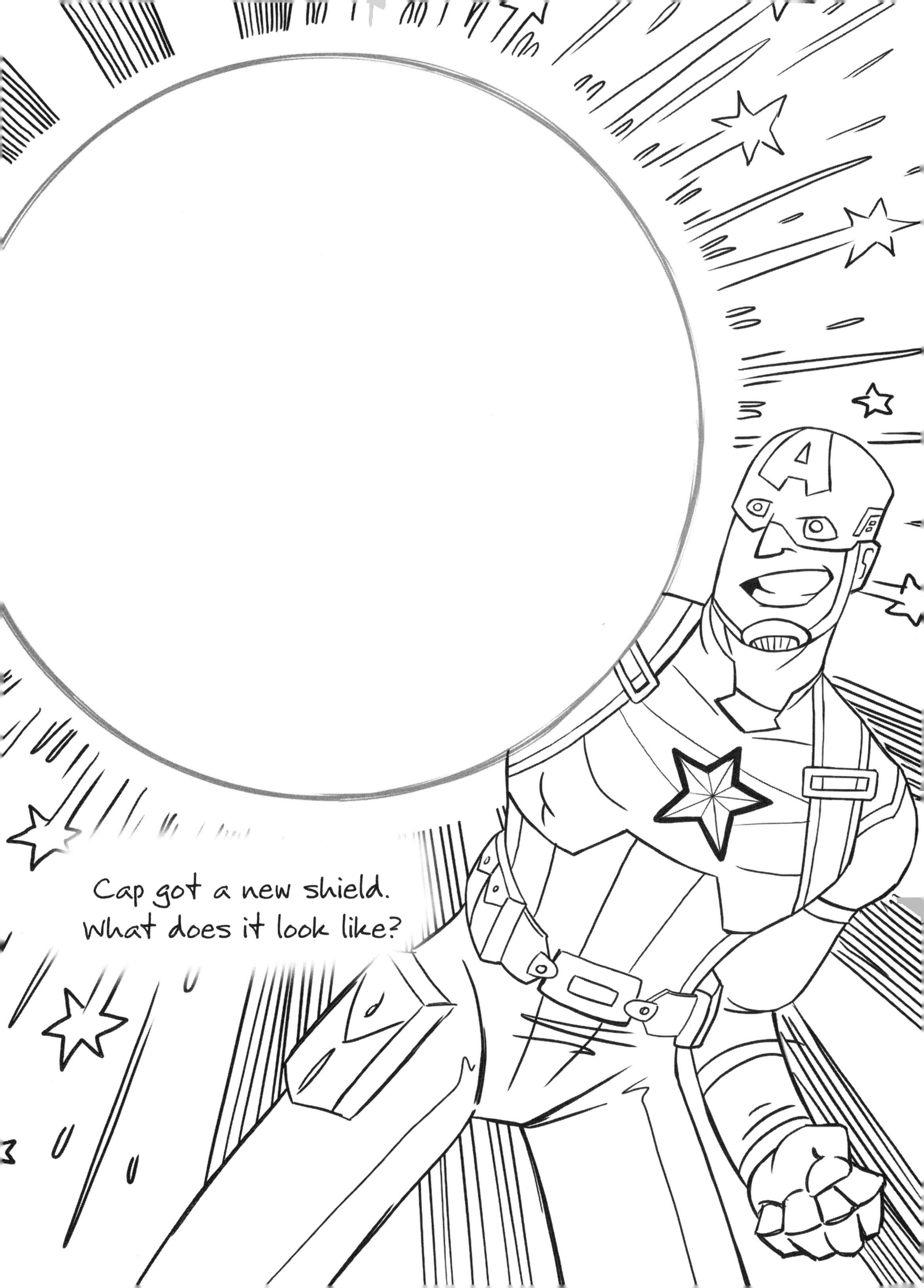
Cap got a new shield.
What does it look like?

Falcon needs some new wings.
Draw them!

10

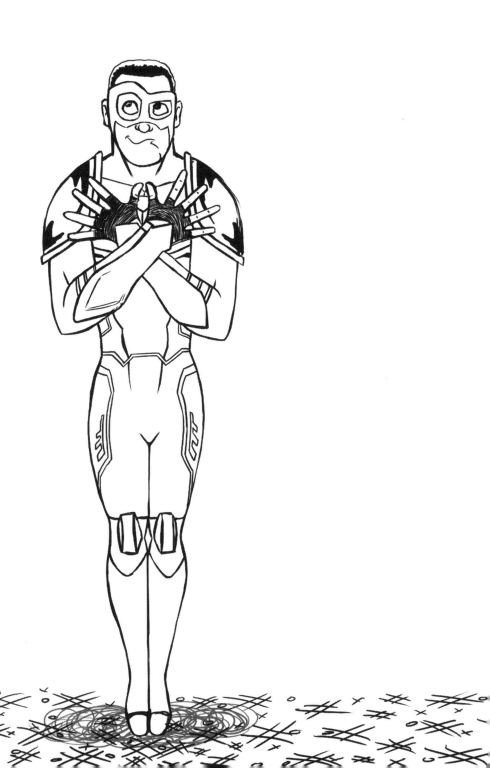

Spider-Man wants a new pattern on his costume.
Make it look AWESOME!

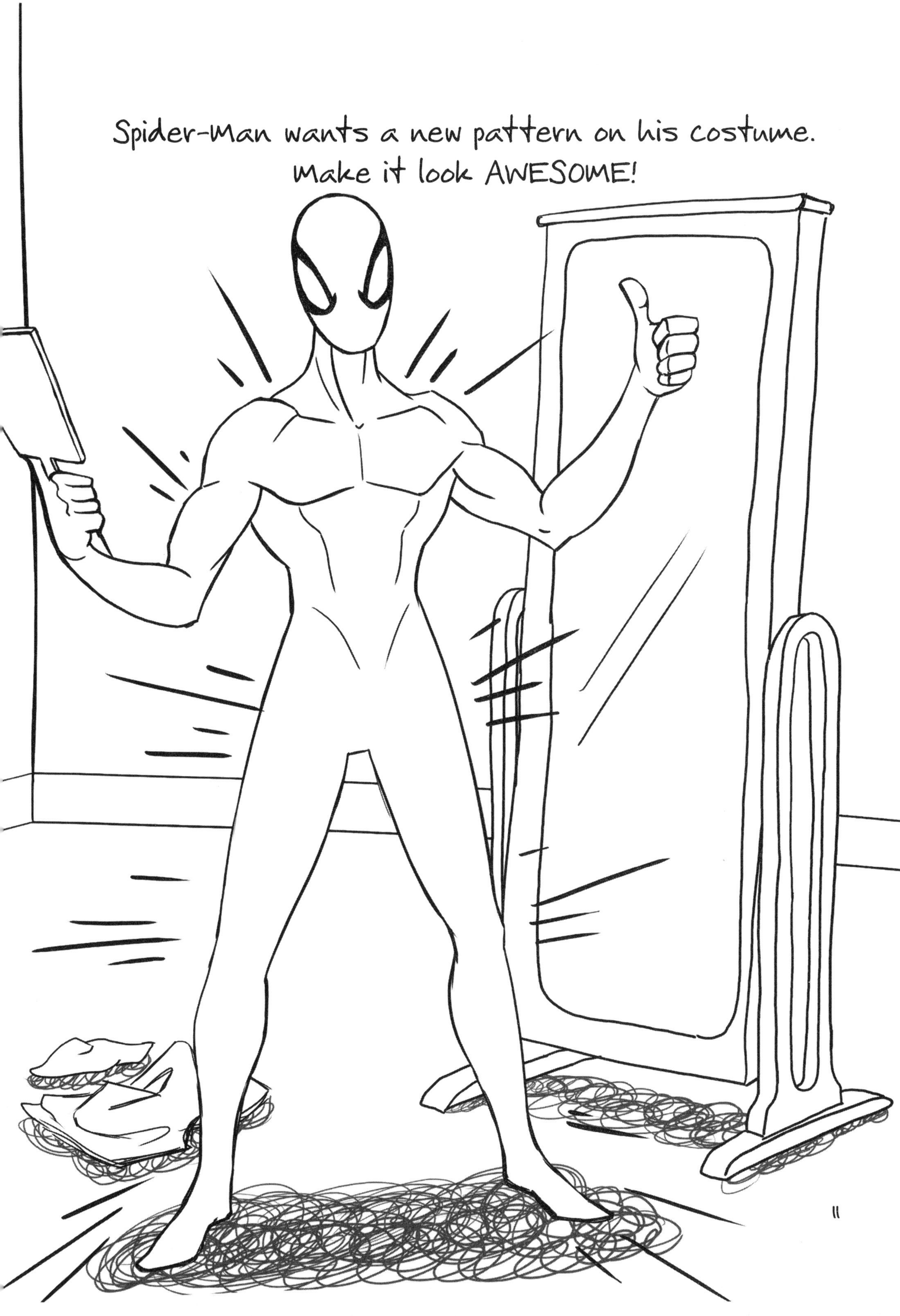

Rocket accidentally crashed the Milano, and the Guardians of the Galaxy have to use a replacement.

Draw in the new ship!

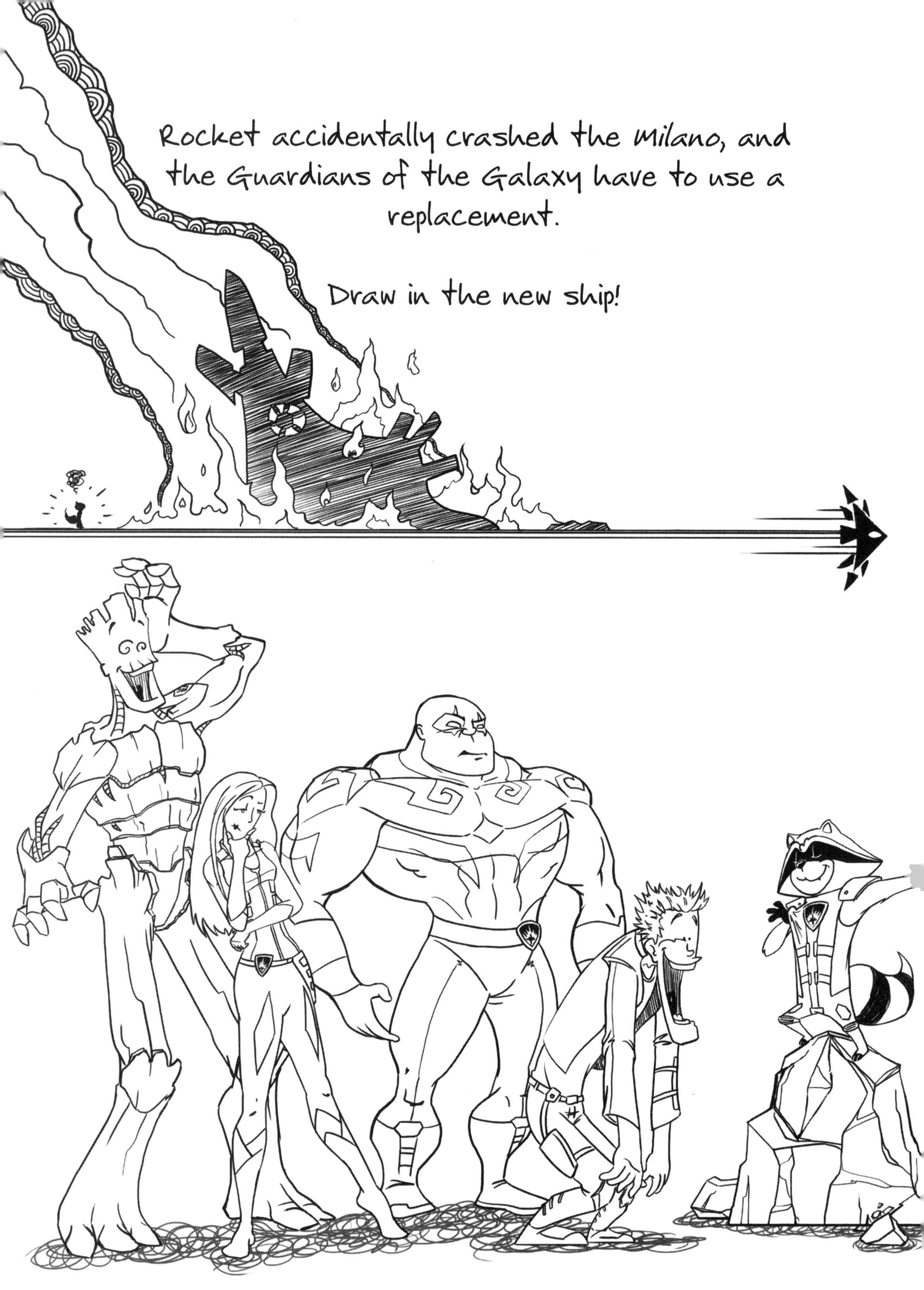

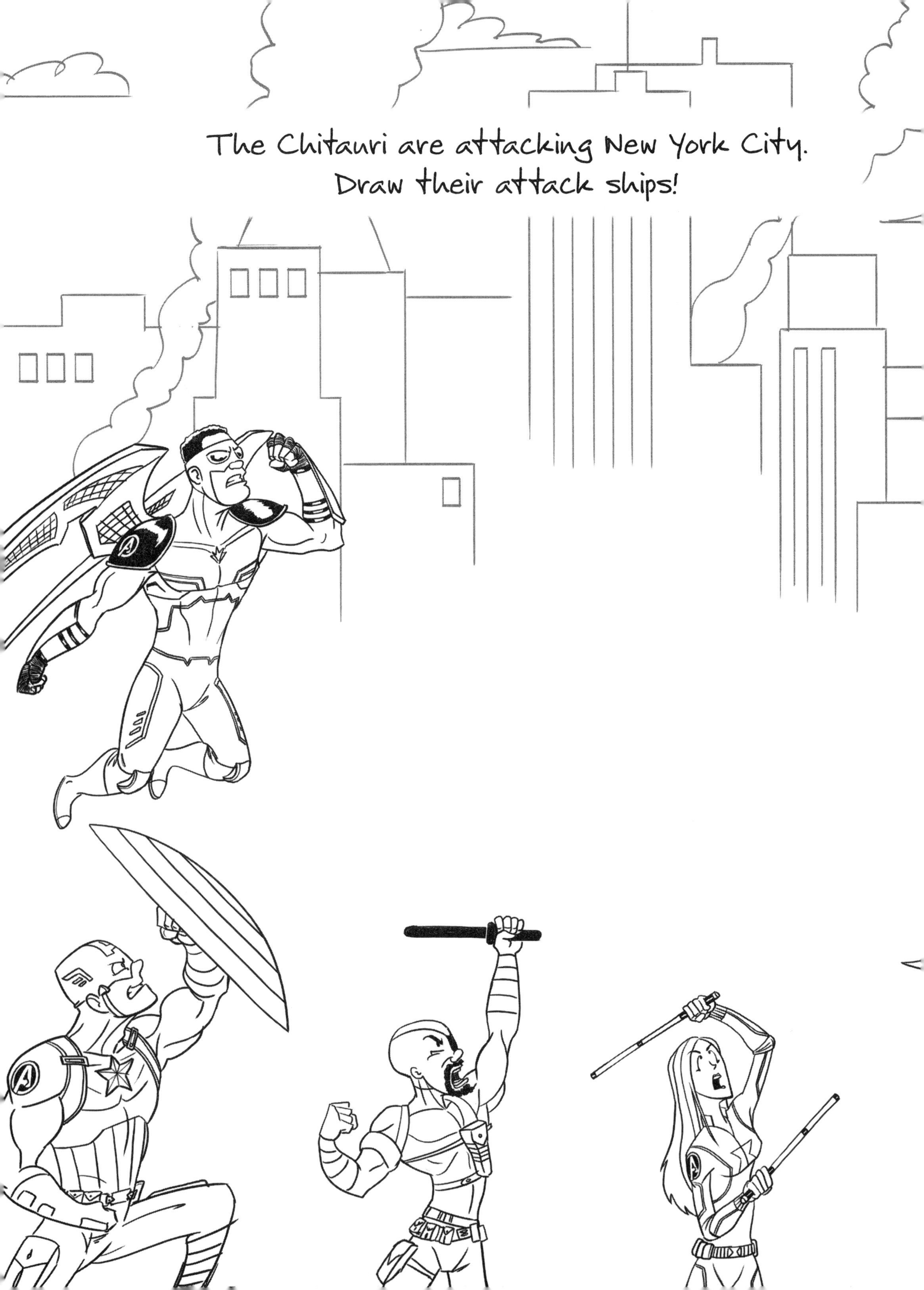
The Chitauri are attacking New York City.
Draw their attack ships!

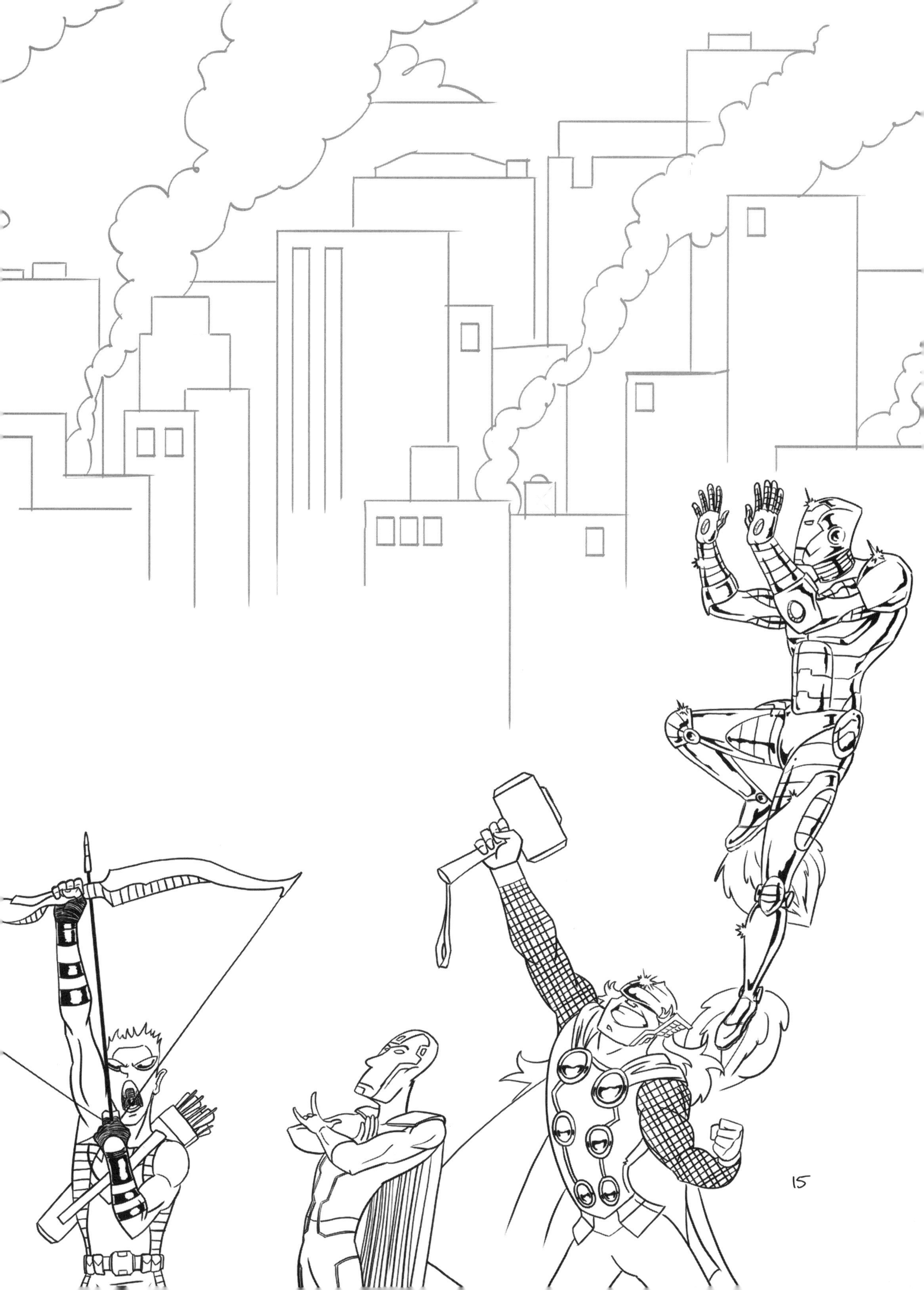

Black Widow wants a new hairdo.
Draw her one.

Hulk wants a new hairdo, too!

Star-Lord got new headphones.
What do they look like?

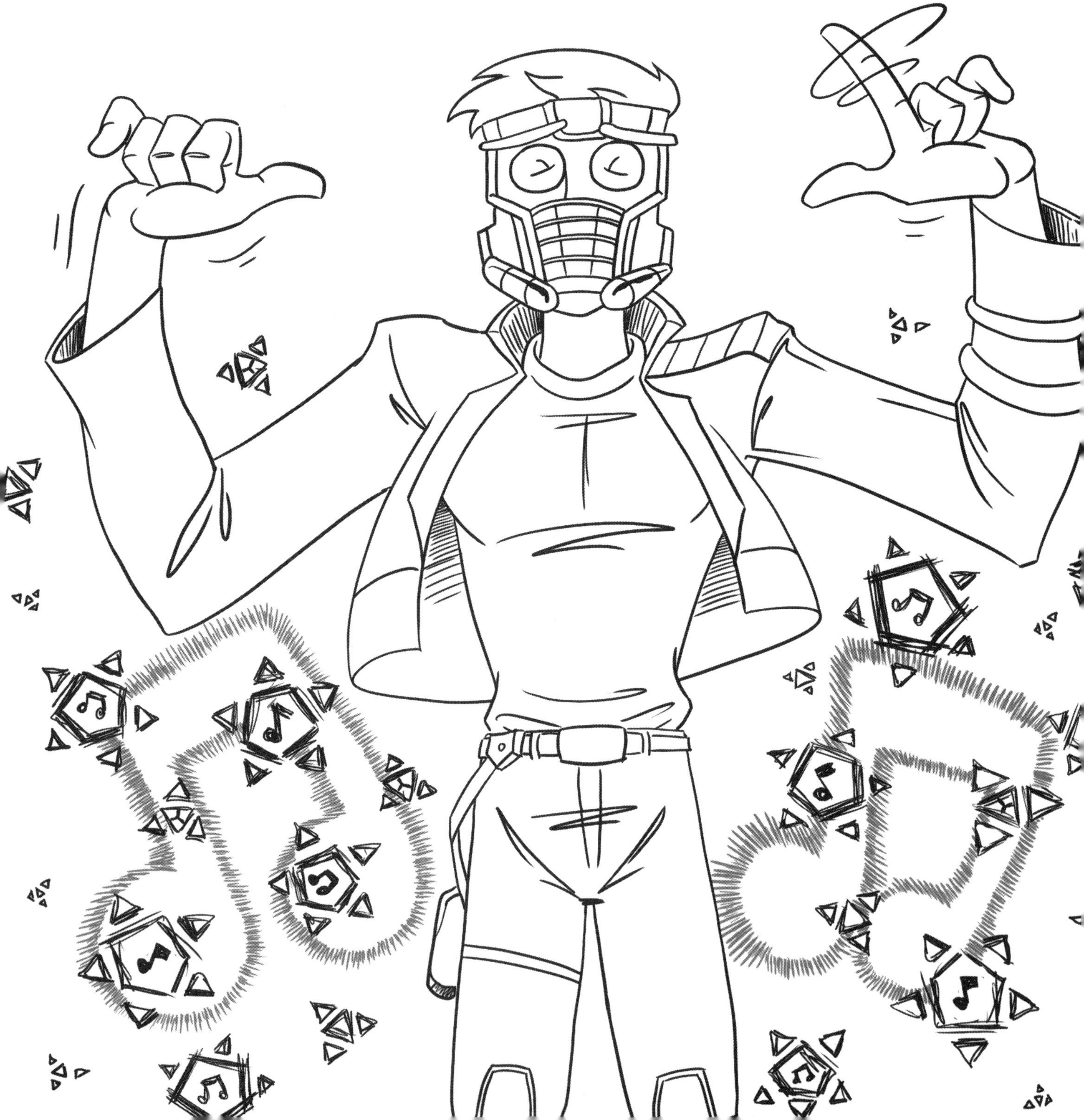

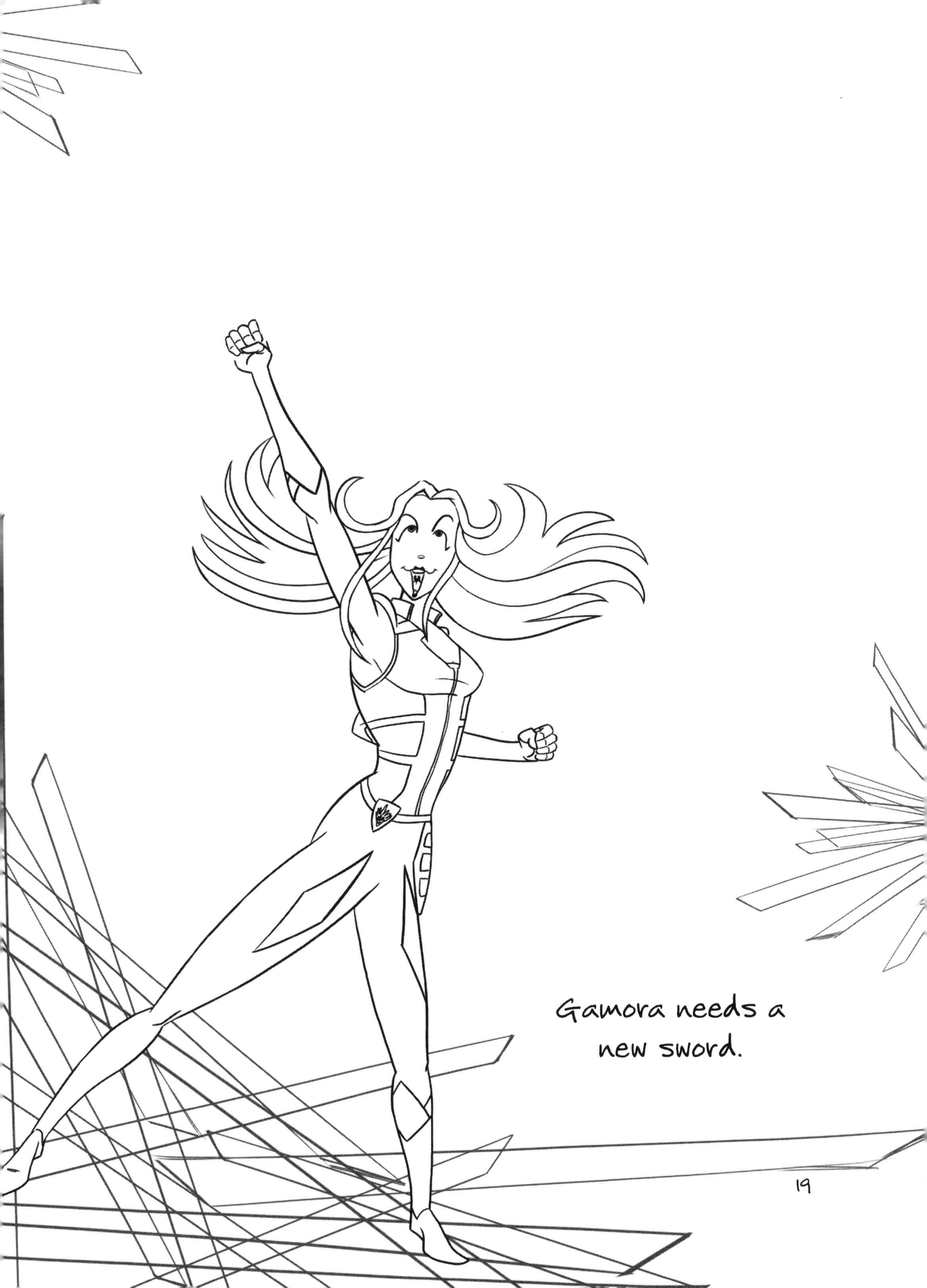

Gamora needs a
new sword.

Draw Groot growing from this pot.

What is Hulk smashing?

Draw Black Widow's cool new ride.

Ultron needs a new body.
What should it look like?

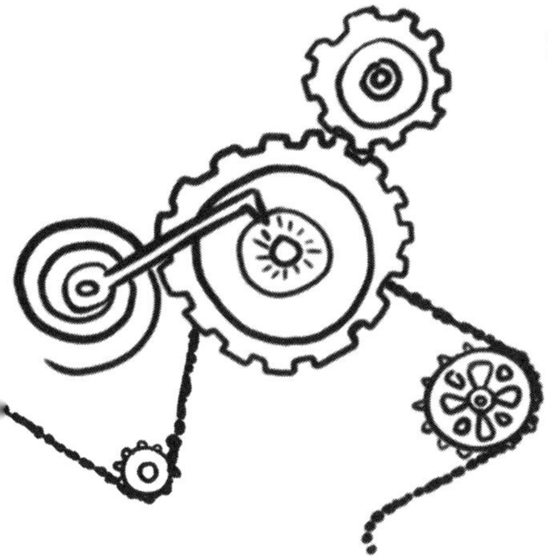

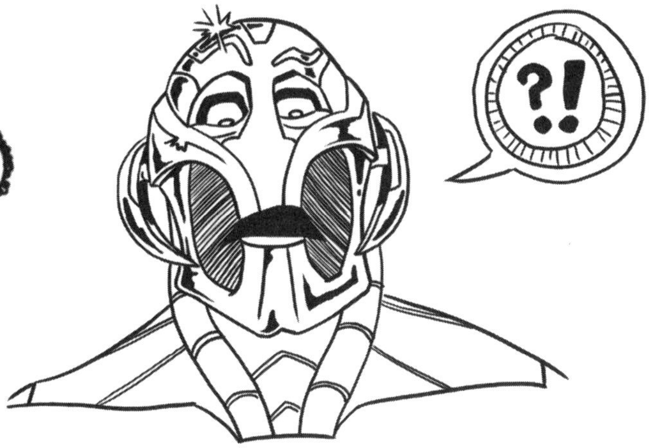
?!

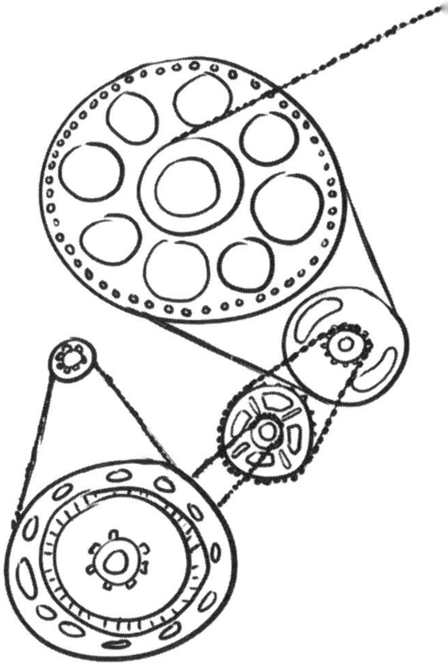

Thor has lost his hammer.
Which tool should he use instead?

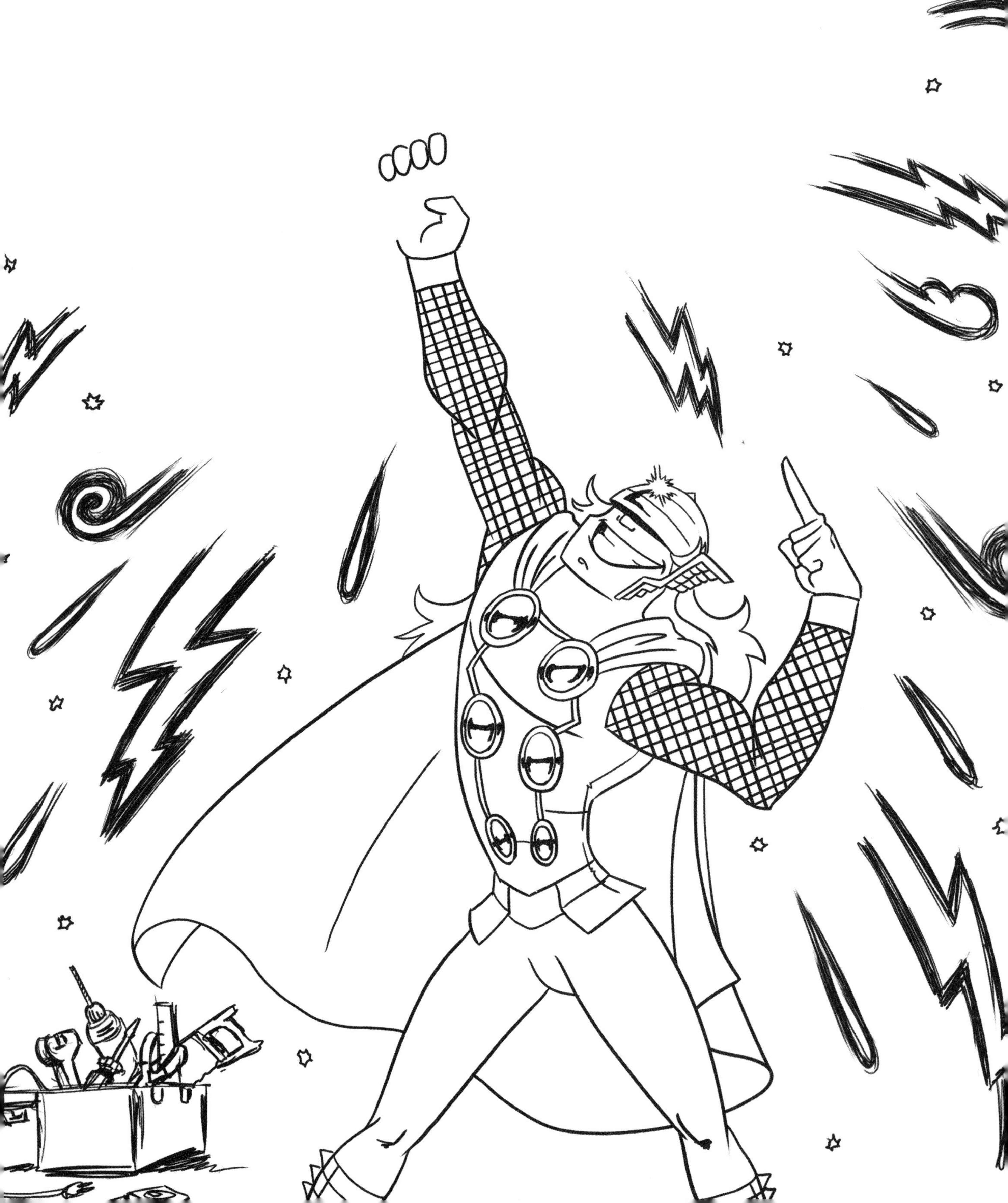

What is Spider-Man
hanging from?

Hawkeye is practicing shooting his arrows.
How many arrows have hit the targets?

Draw Asgard's beautiful skyline.

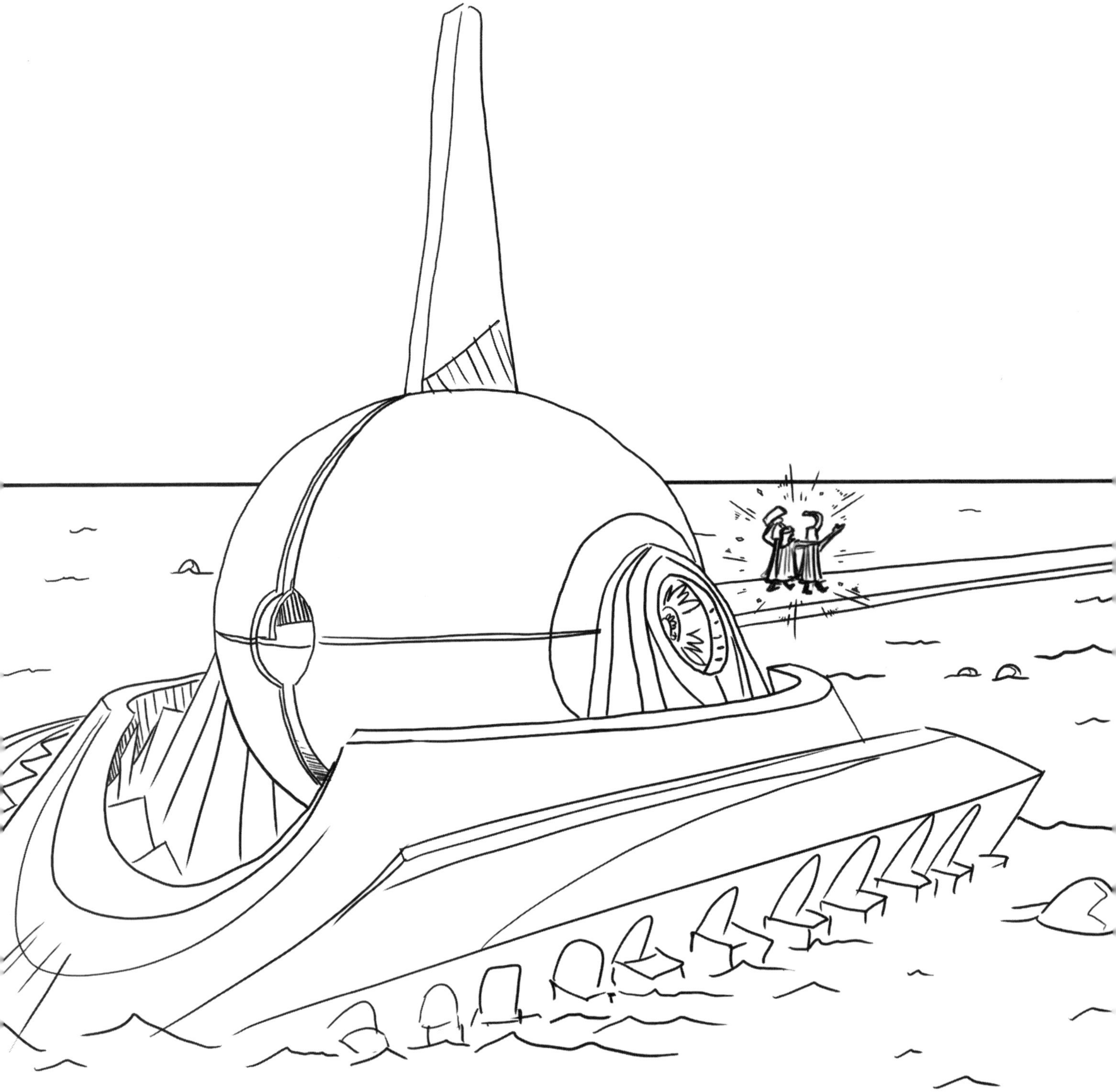

The Guardians of the Galaxy are being
chased by Yondu's ships.
Draw how many ships are chasing them!

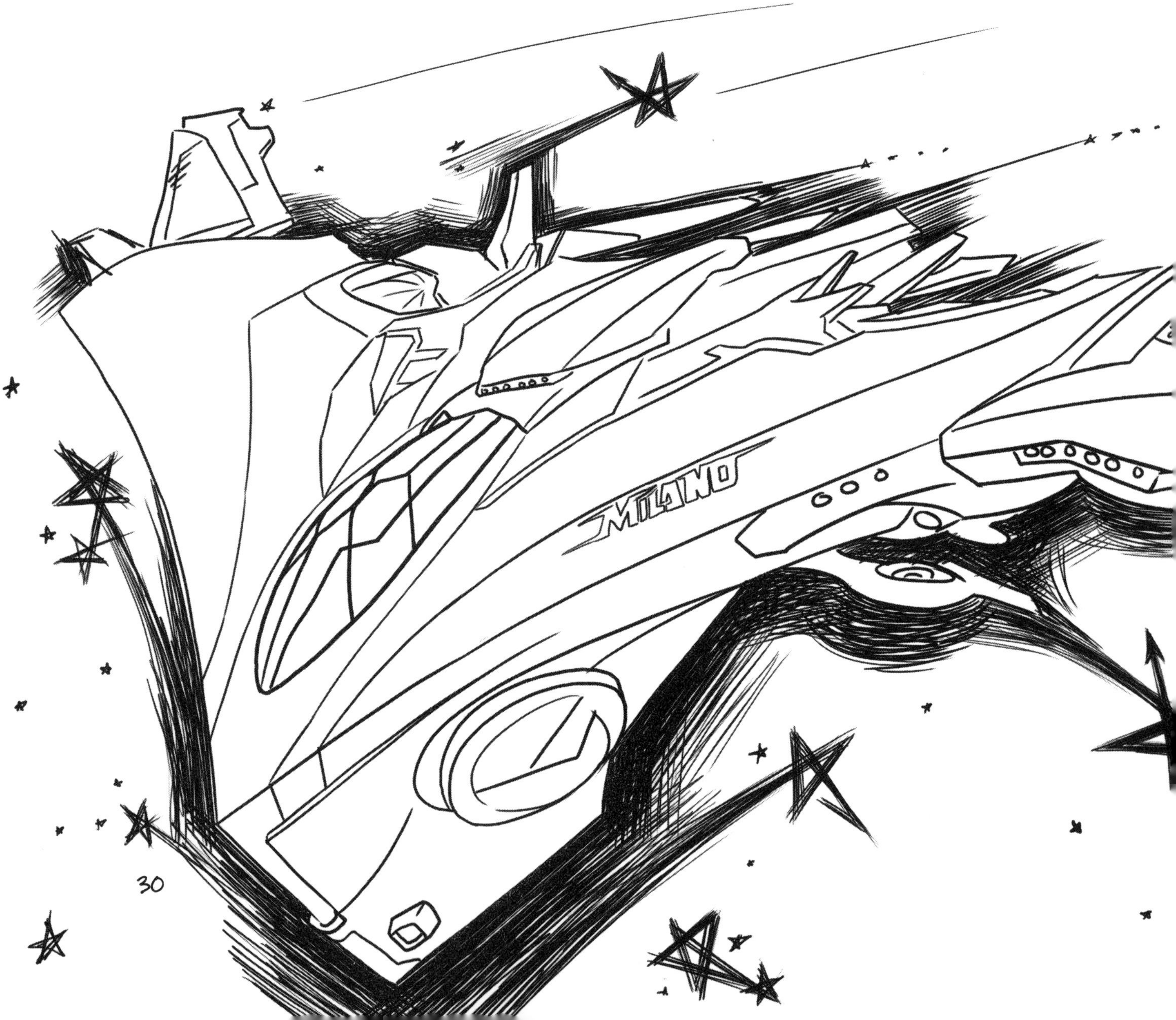
MILANO

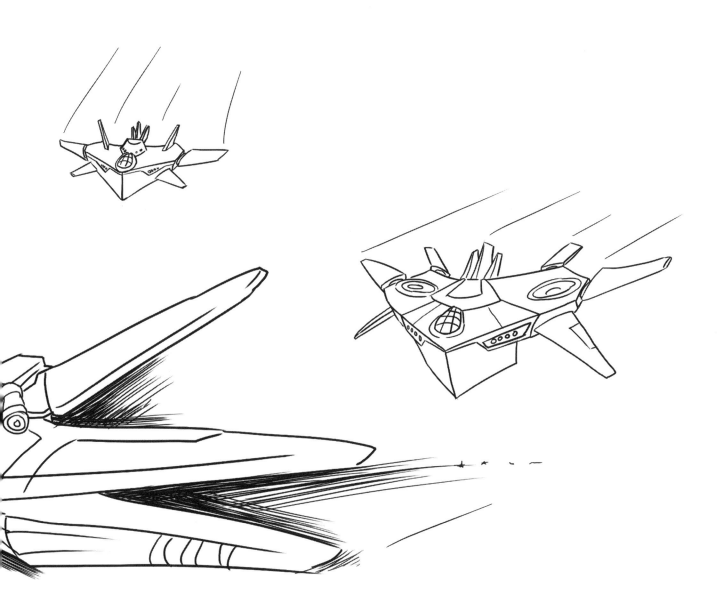

Loki is up to no good again.
What mischief has he caused this time?

Arnim Zola wants to grow a mustache.
Draw him a good one.

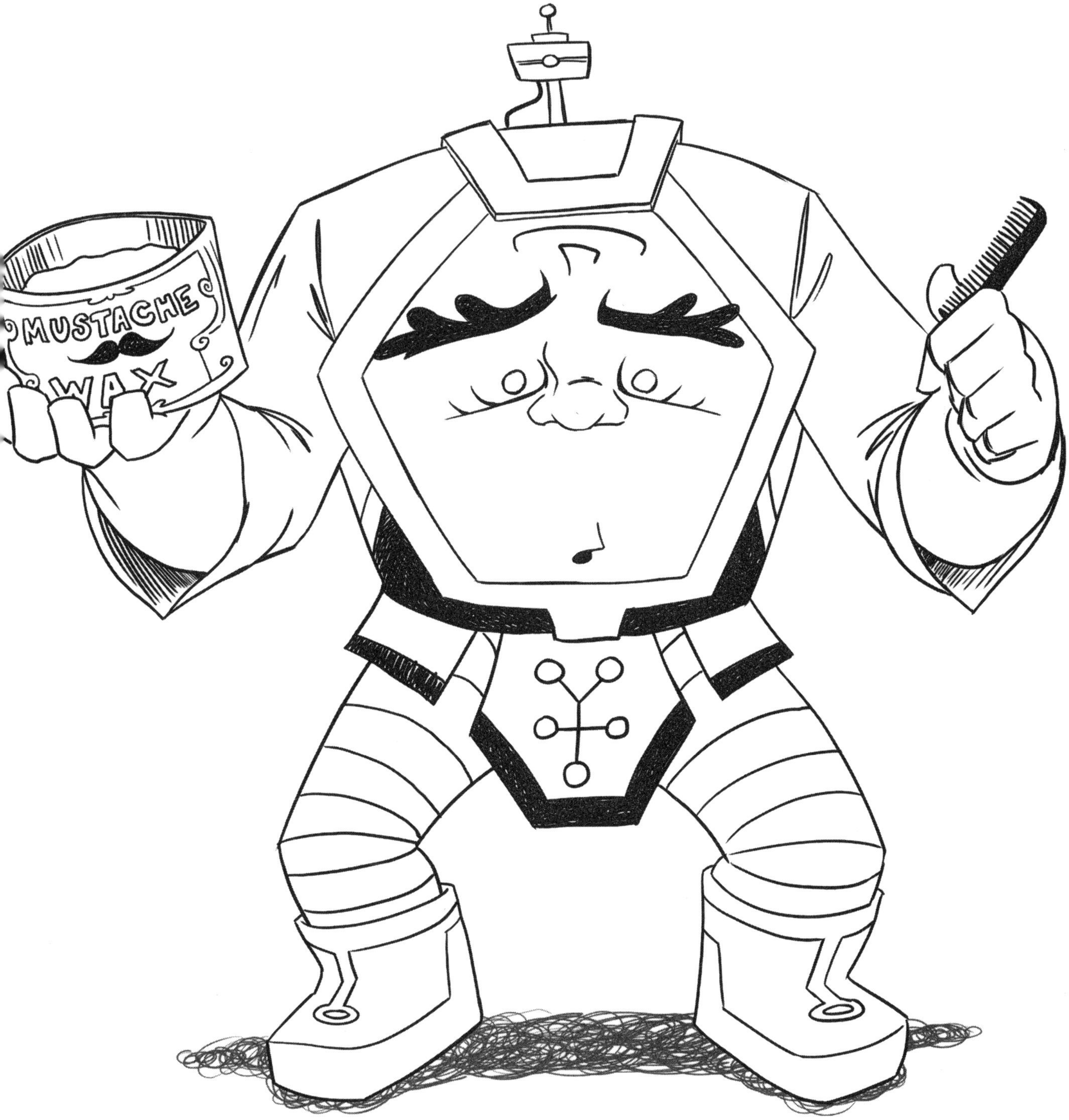
MUSTACHE
WAX

The *Milano* has lost a wing. Draw in a replacement.

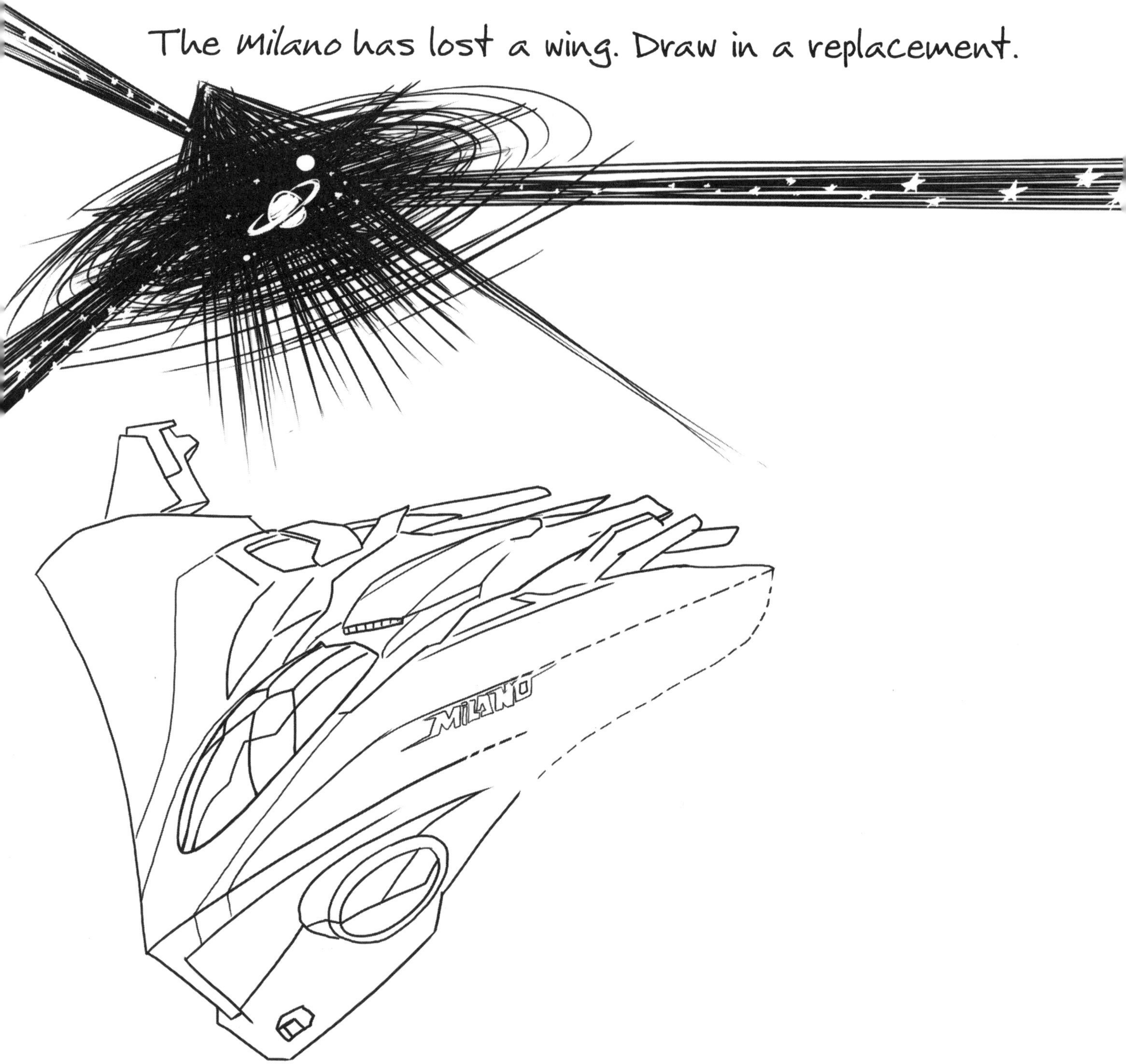
MILANO

Iron Man has new Hulkbuster armor.
What does it look like?

The Avengers are out for dinner.
Iron Man ordered shawarma.

What did everyone else order?

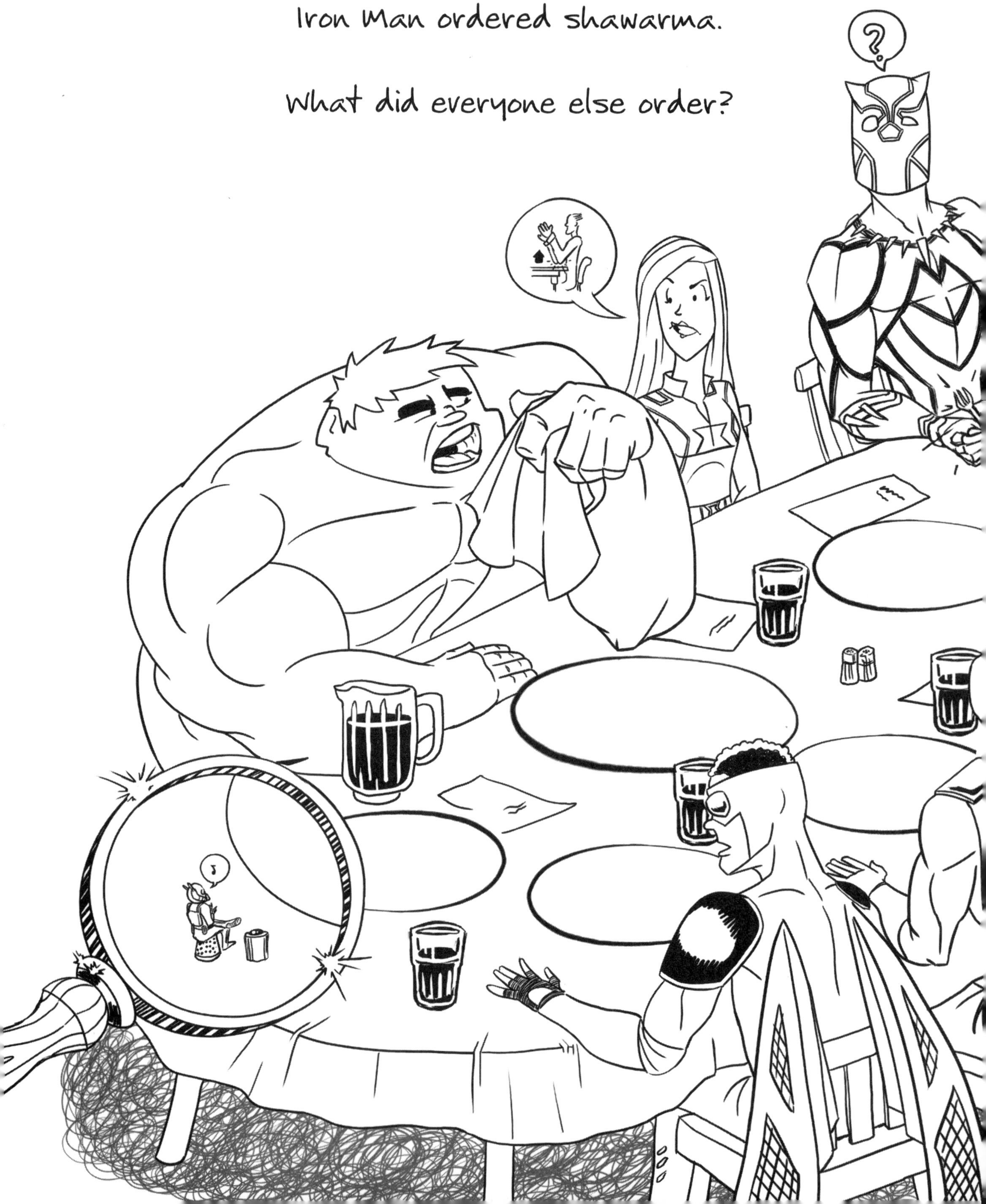
?

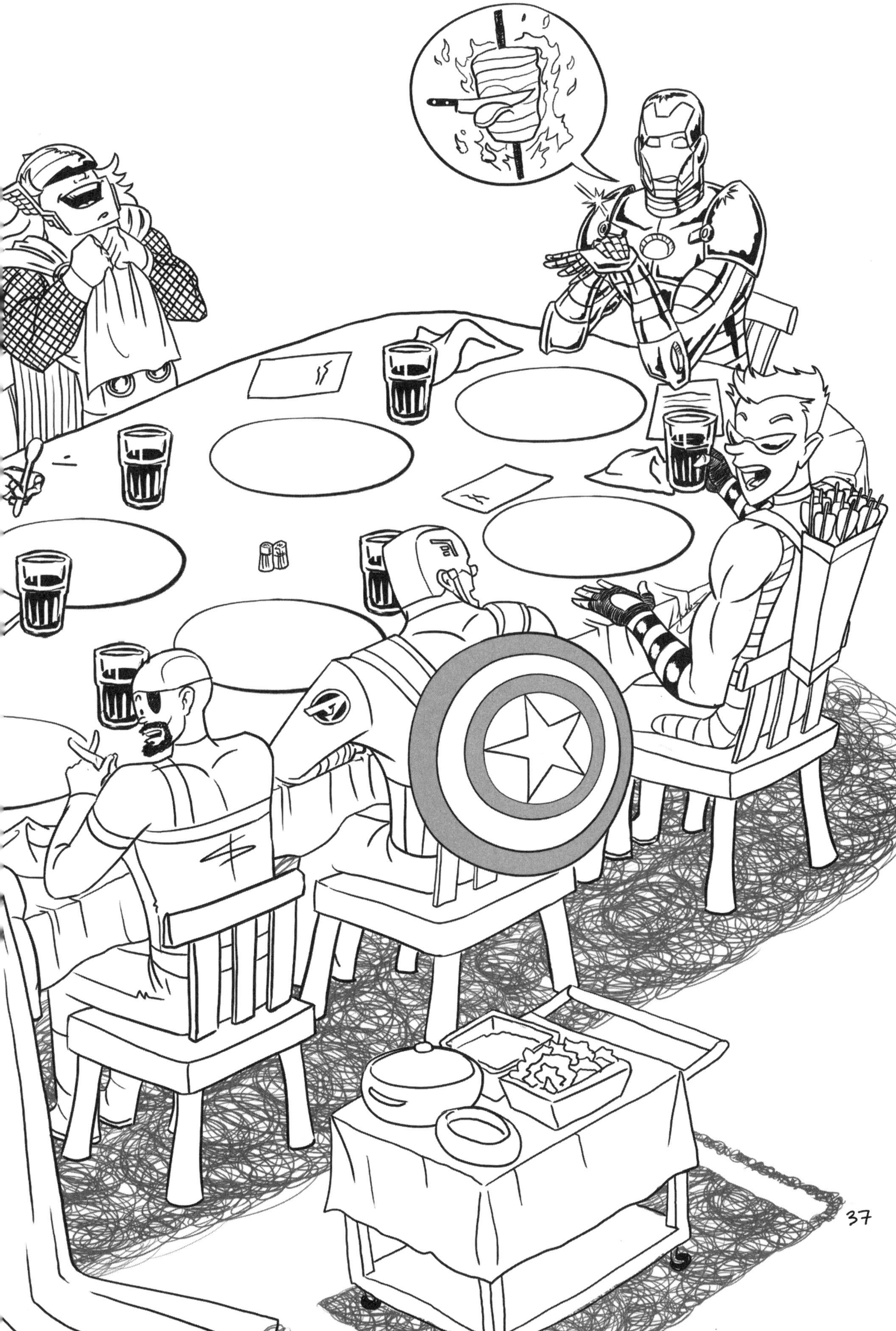

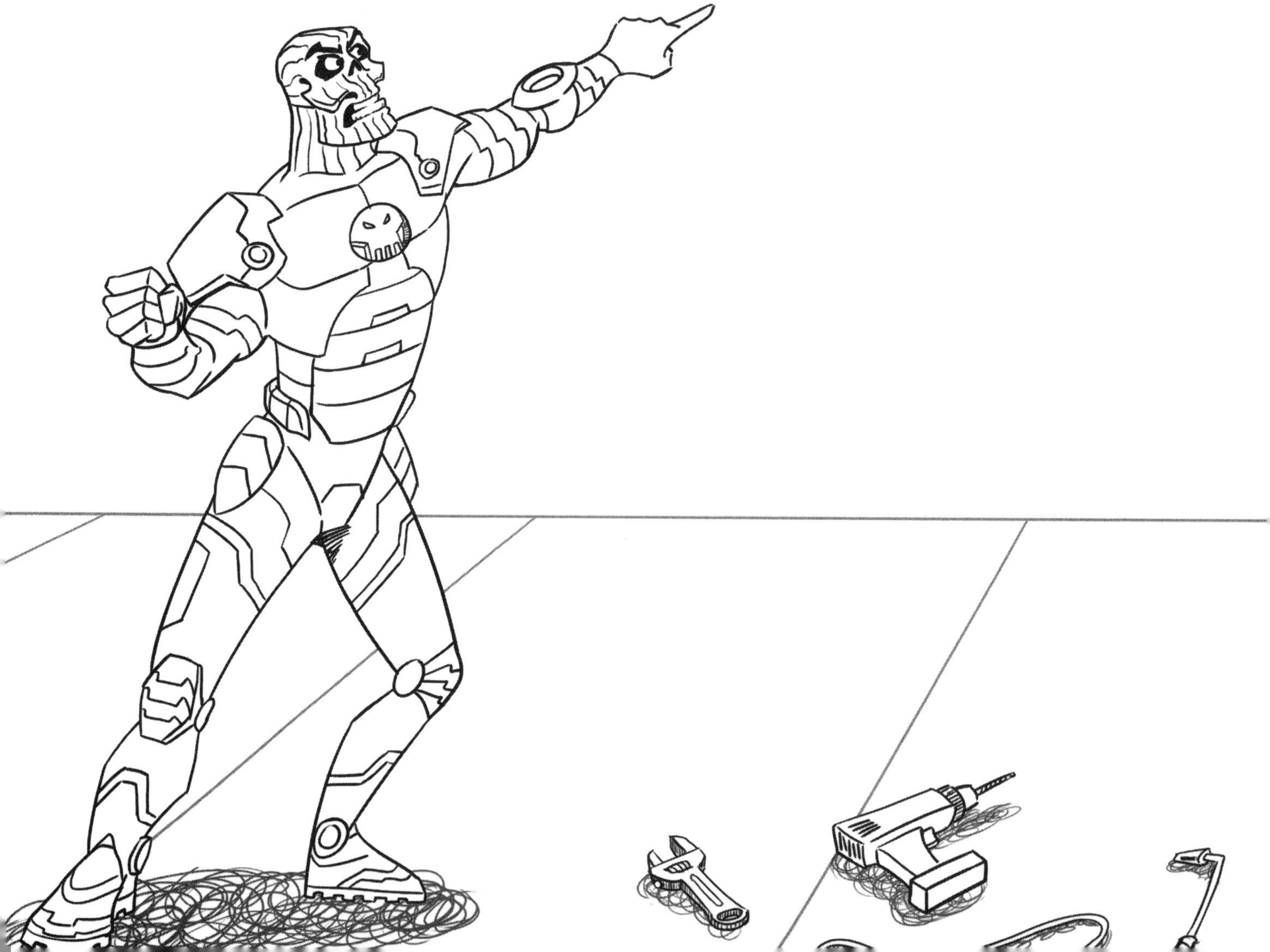

Red Skull has a new device to dominate the world.
What does it look like?

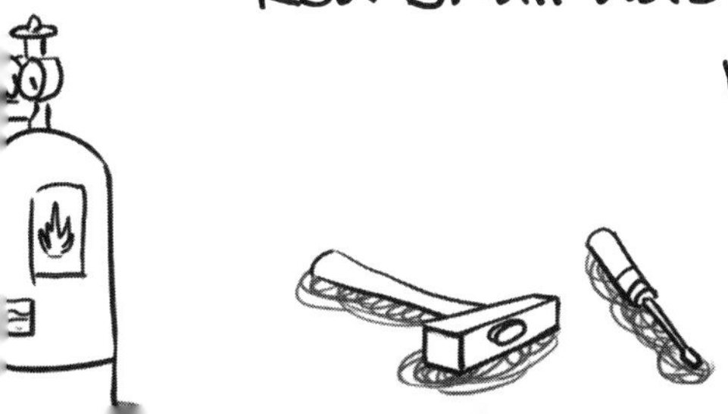

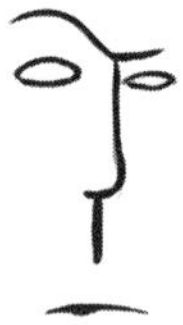

Check it out! Vision is invisible.
The page is blank. We know.
Draw whatever you like!

What is in Peter Parker's locker?
Draw some things!

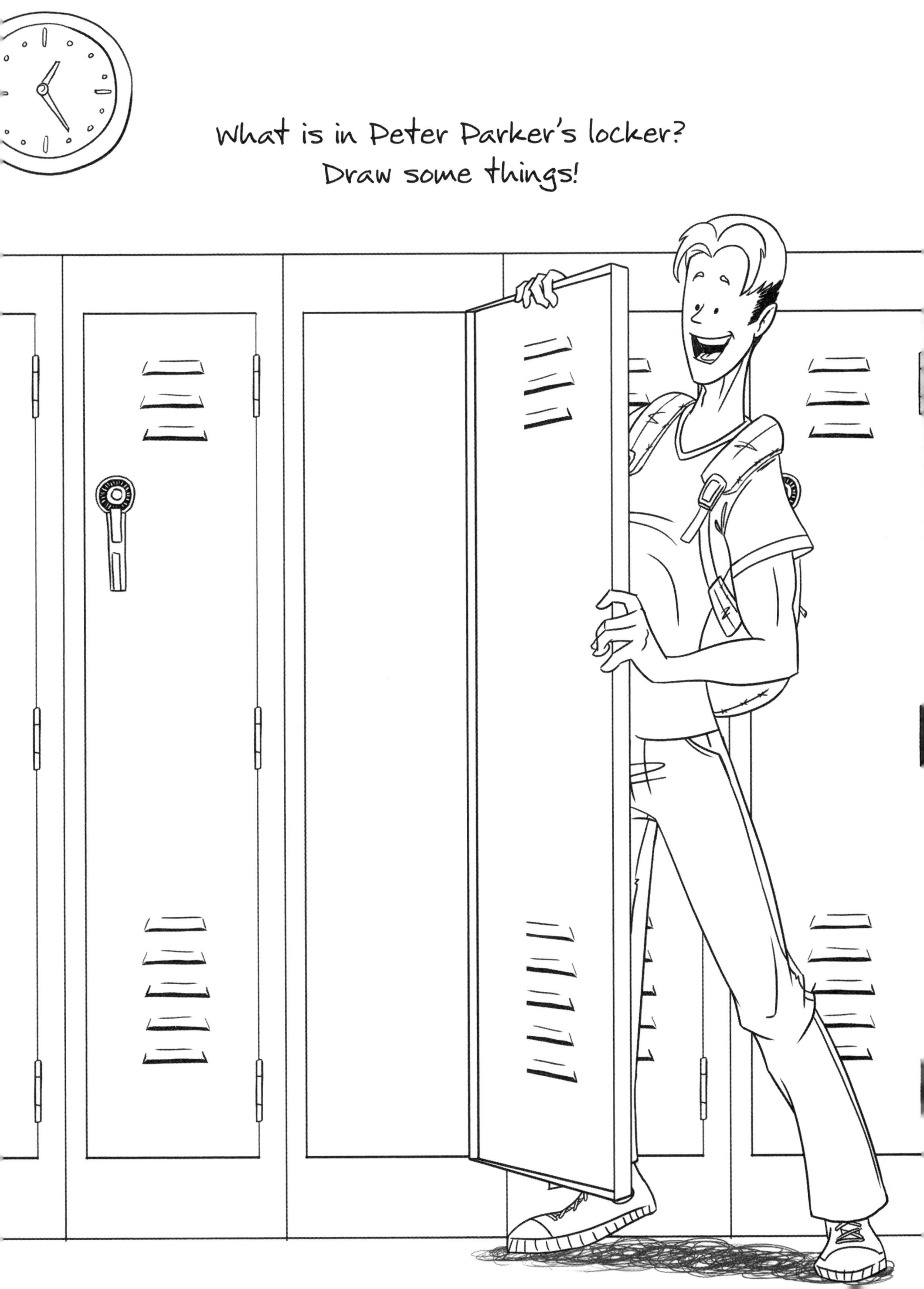

Doctor Octopus has lost his tentacles.
Draw him four new ones.

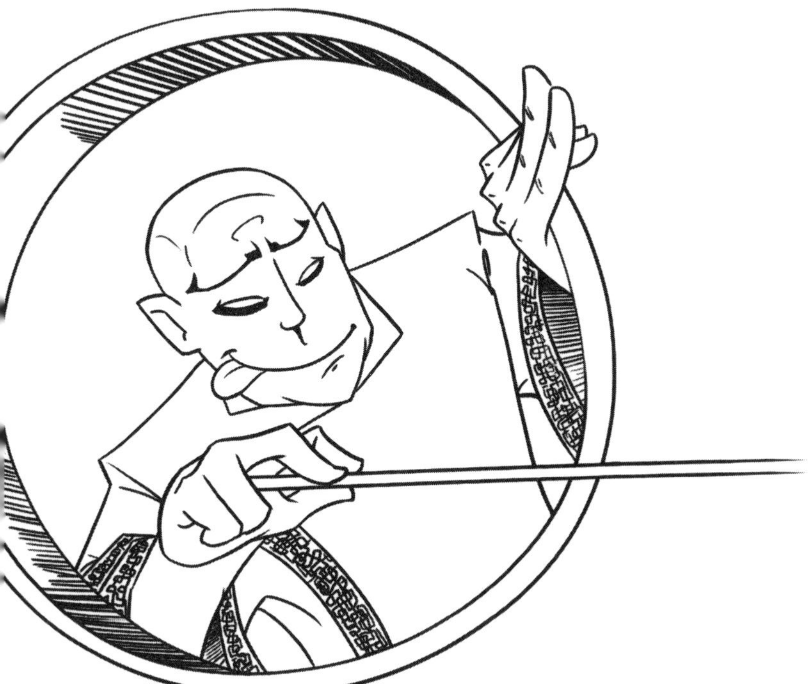

What is Wong roasting over Dormammu's head?

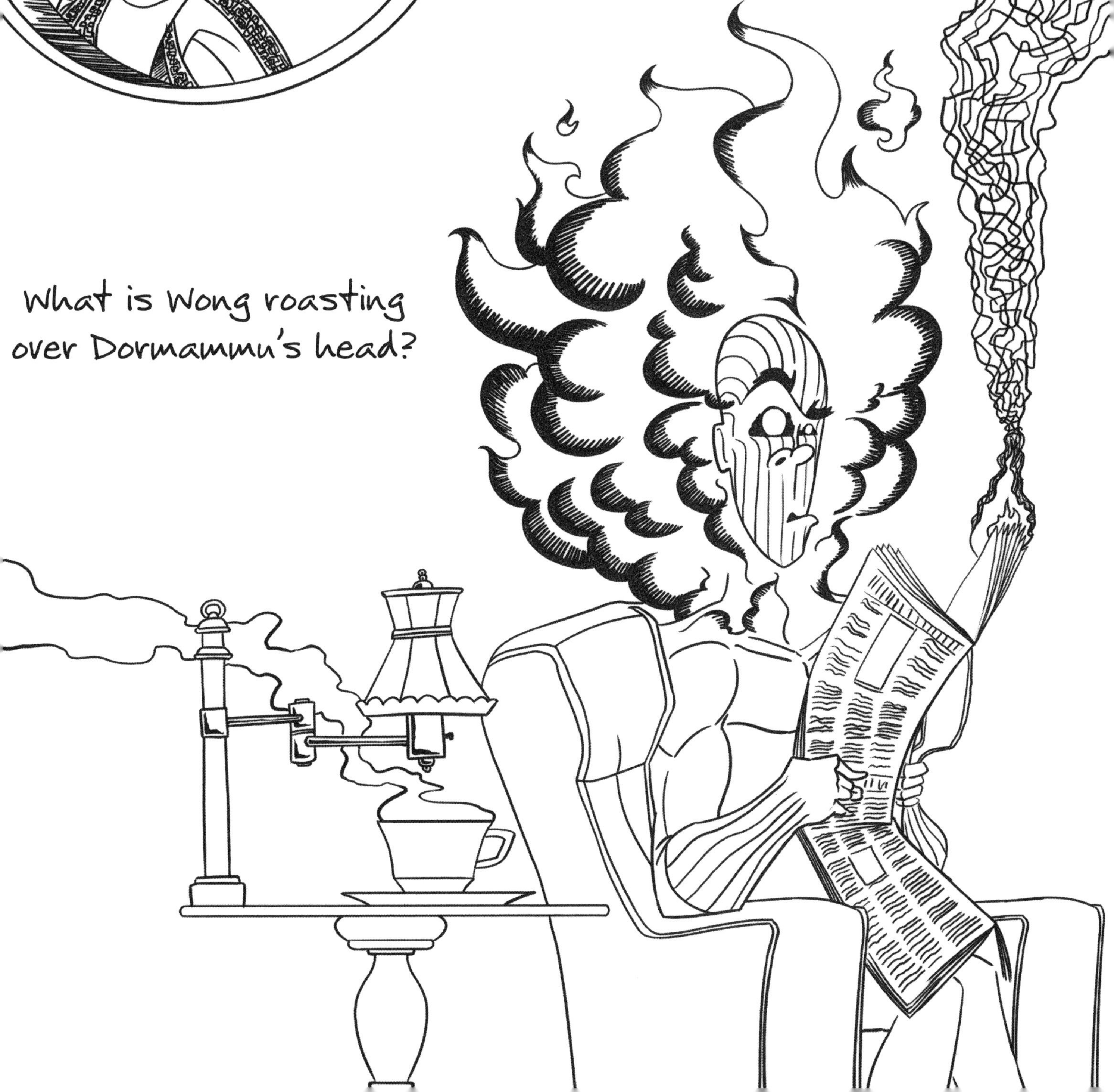

Draw something fast to show
how quick Falcon flies.

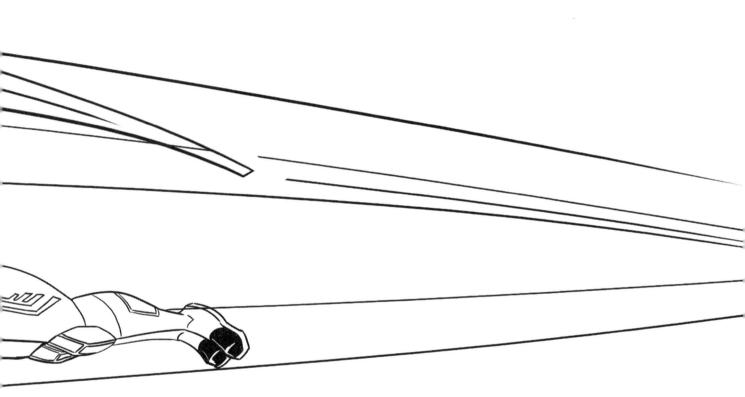

45

Rocket has a cool new ride.
What does it look like?

What is Drax jumping over?

What does the Rainbow Bridge to Asgard look like?

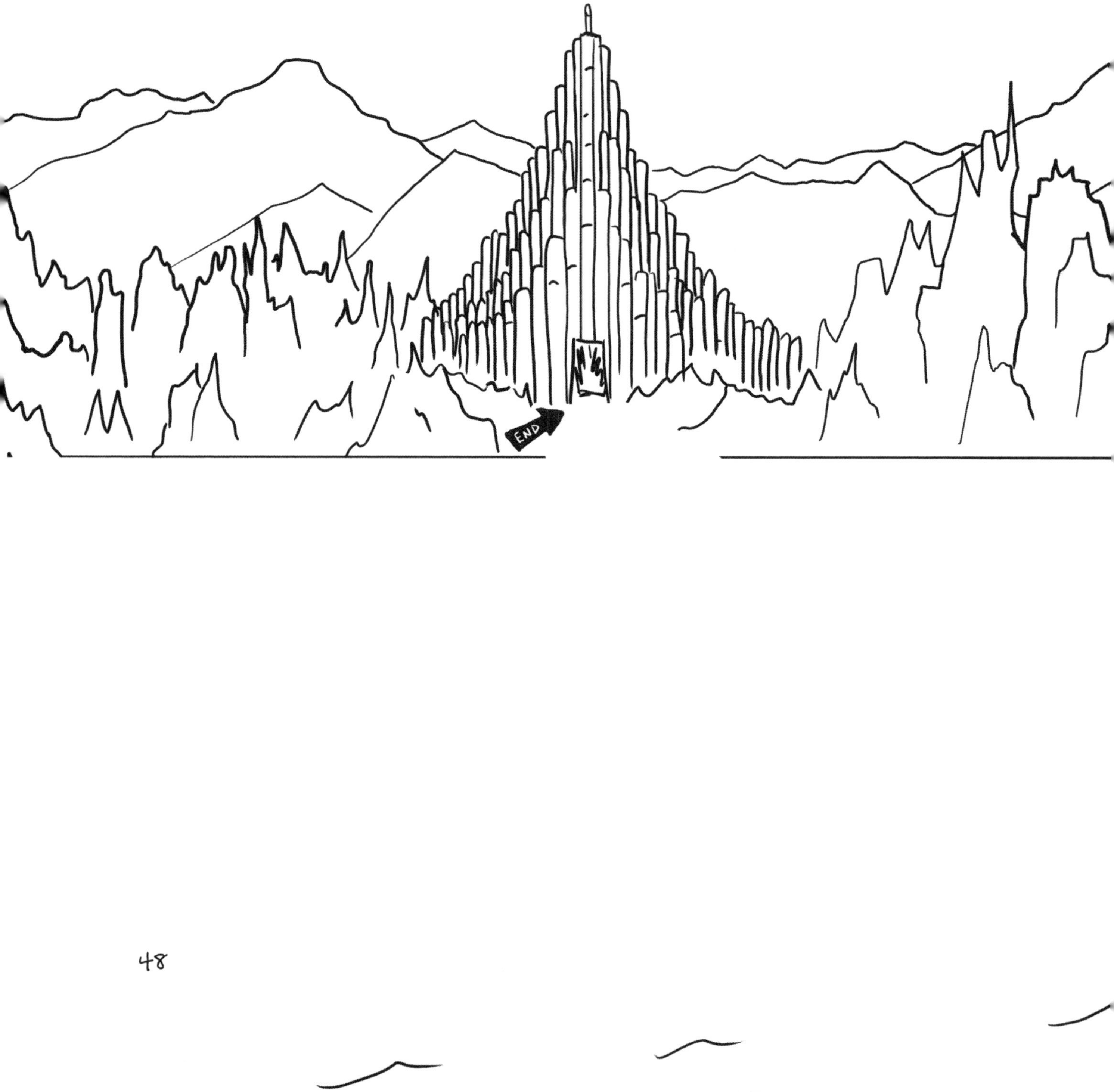
END

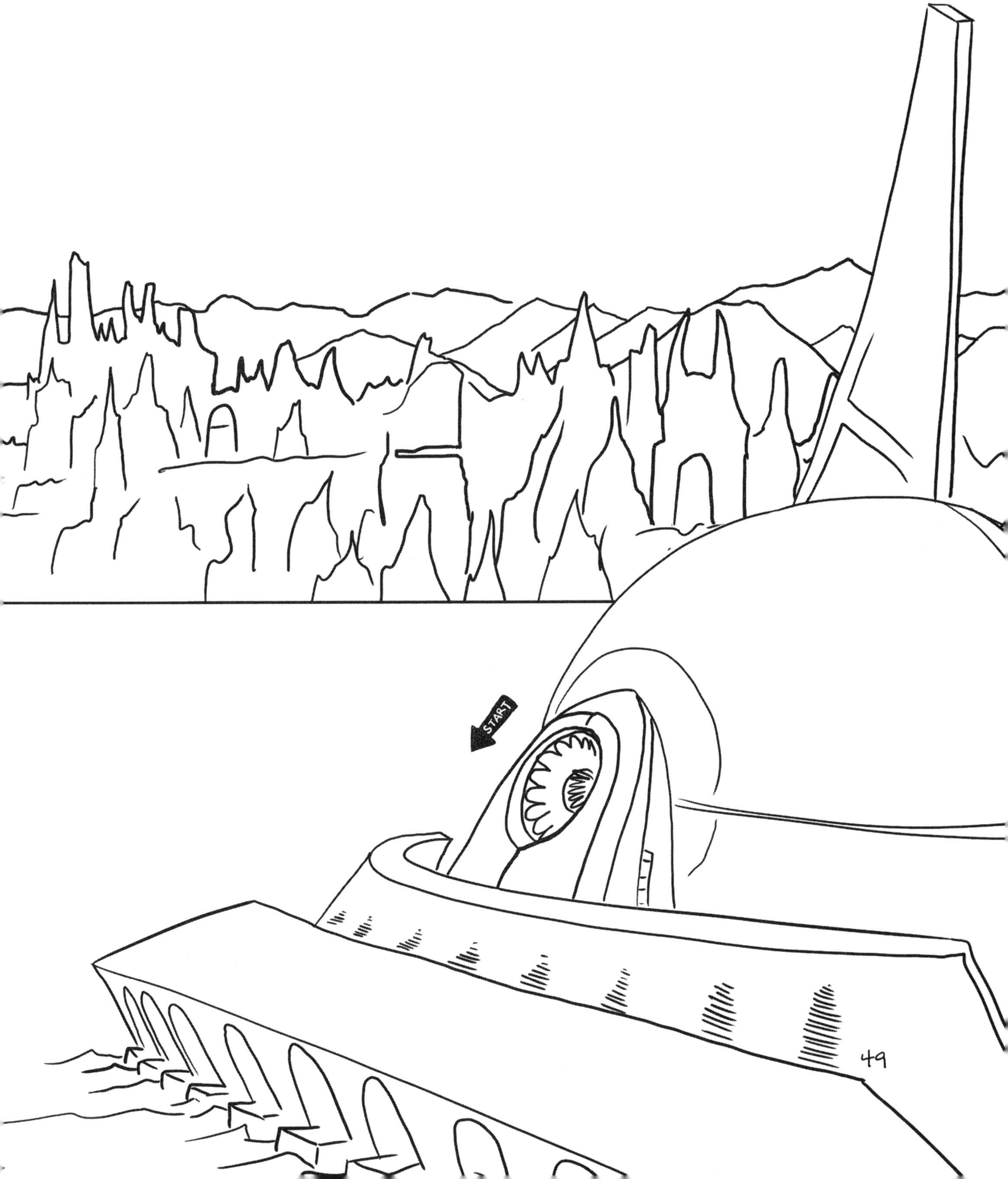
START

Thor has a fancy new cape. Add some cool designs!

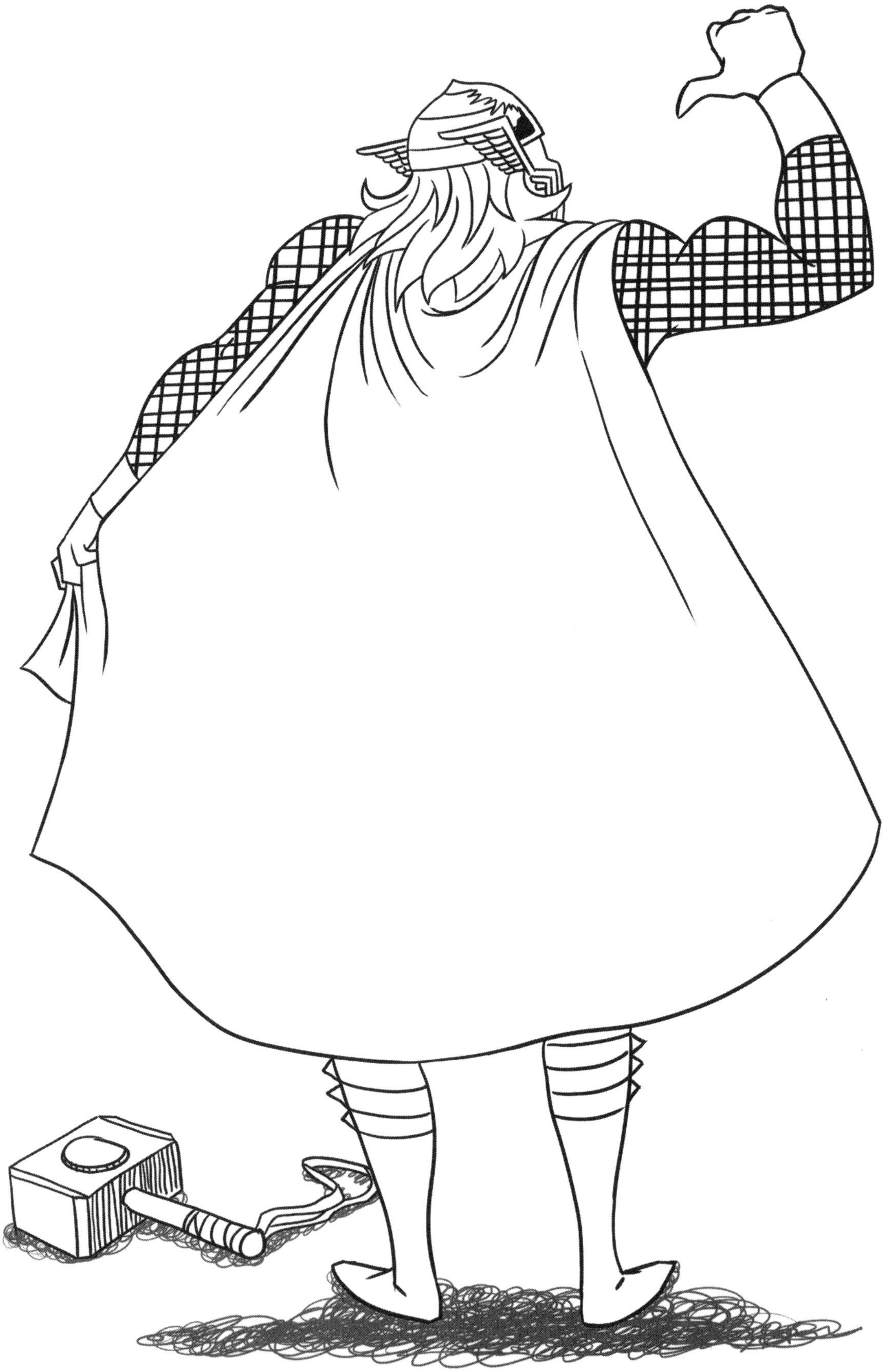

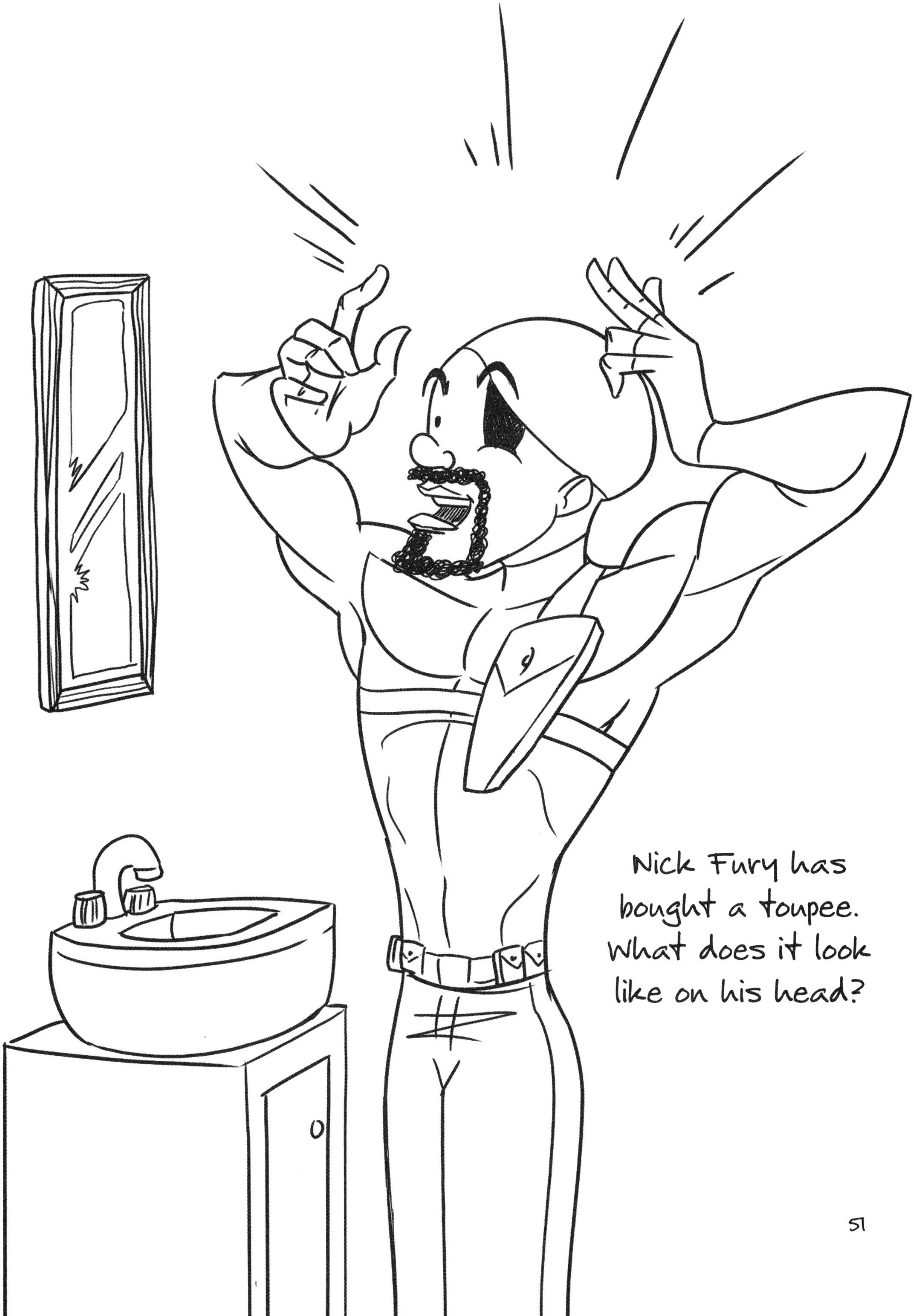

Nick Fury has bought a toupee. What does it look like on his head?

Draw Star-Lord some blaster fire . . .
and what he is blasting!

What has Spider-Man caught in his web?

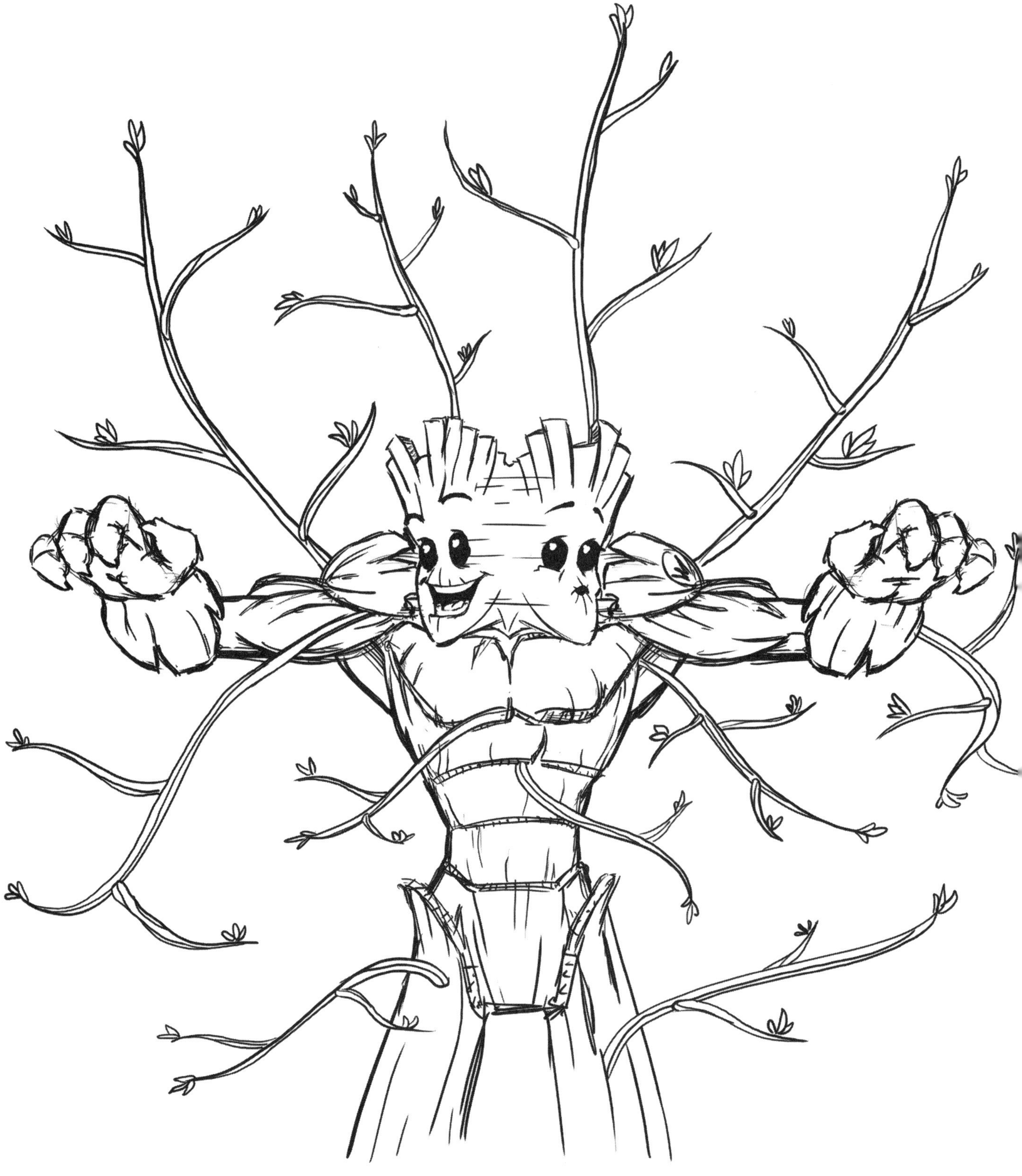

It's spring and Groot has started growing fruit from his limbs. What kind is it?

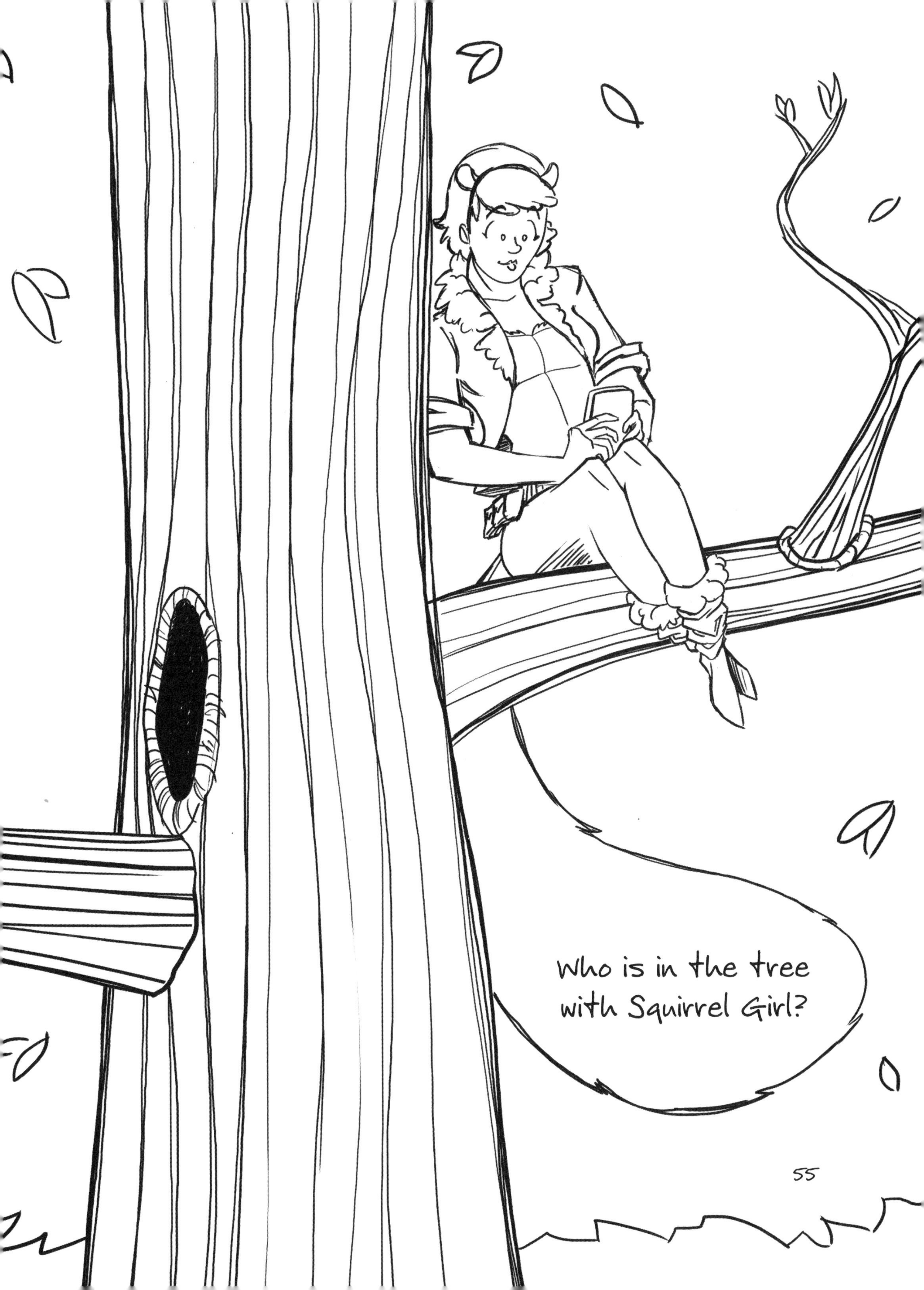
Who is in the tree
with Squirrel Girl?

What did Hulk break this time?
Oh, Hulk.

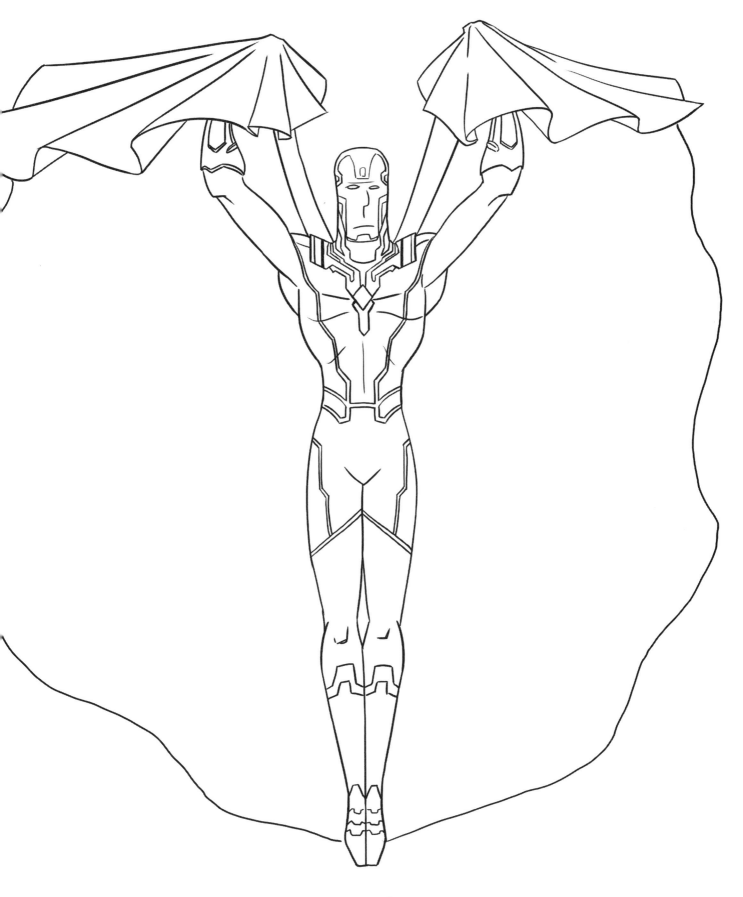

Help Vision decorate his cape.

Draw a helicopter so Spidey can escape
the Sinister Six!

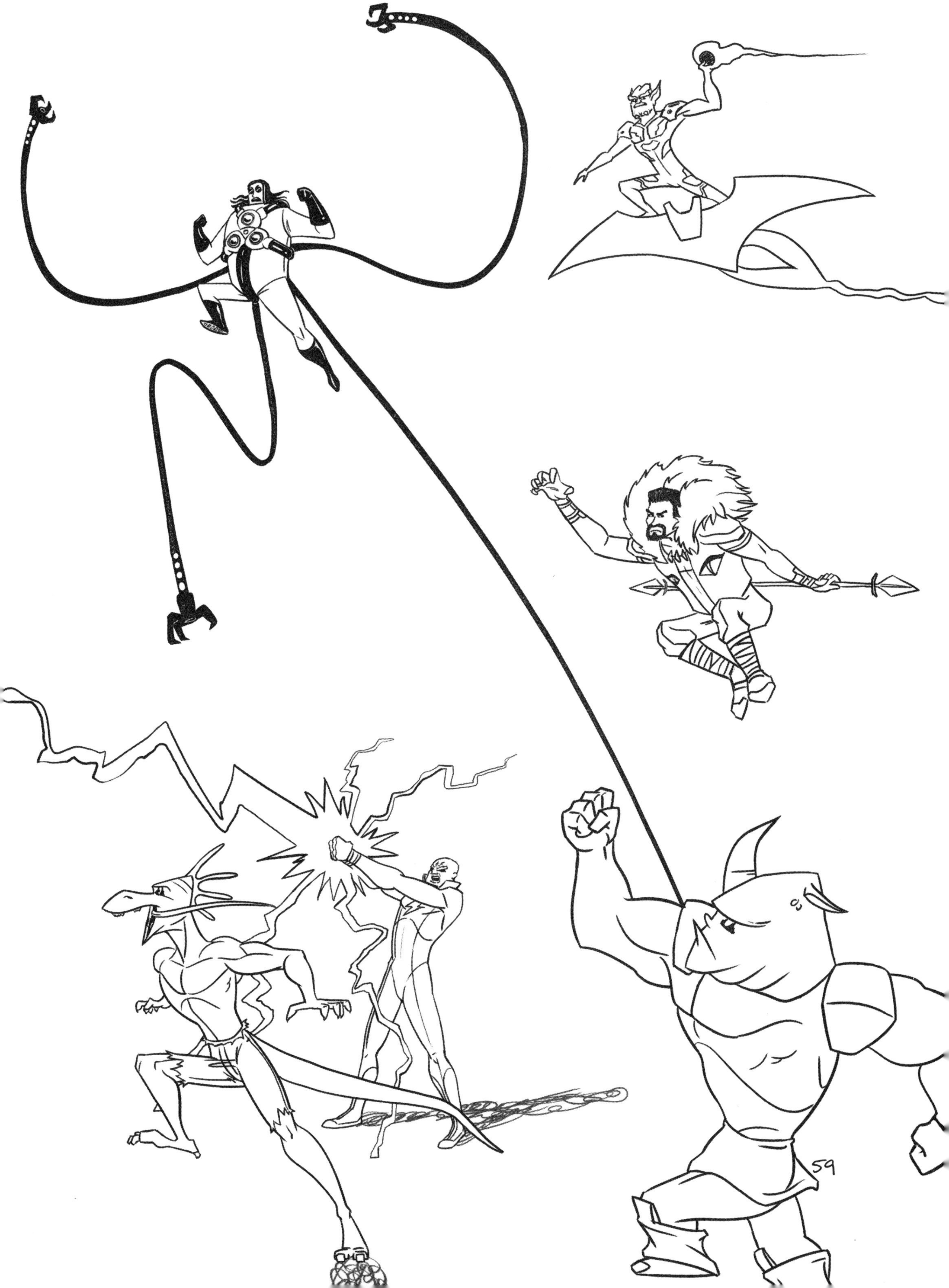

What did Aunt May make for dinner?
It looks like Peter Parker doesn't like it.

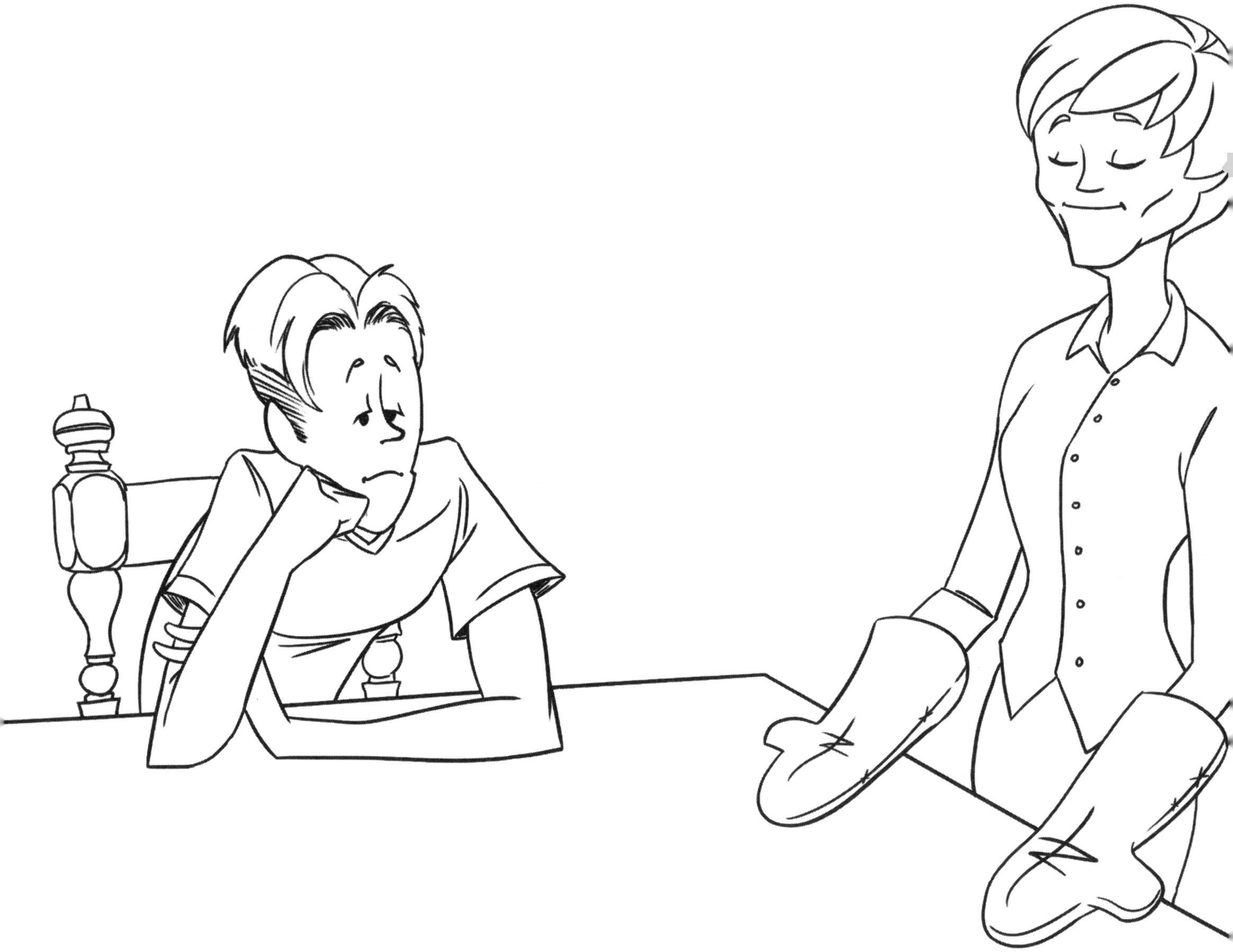

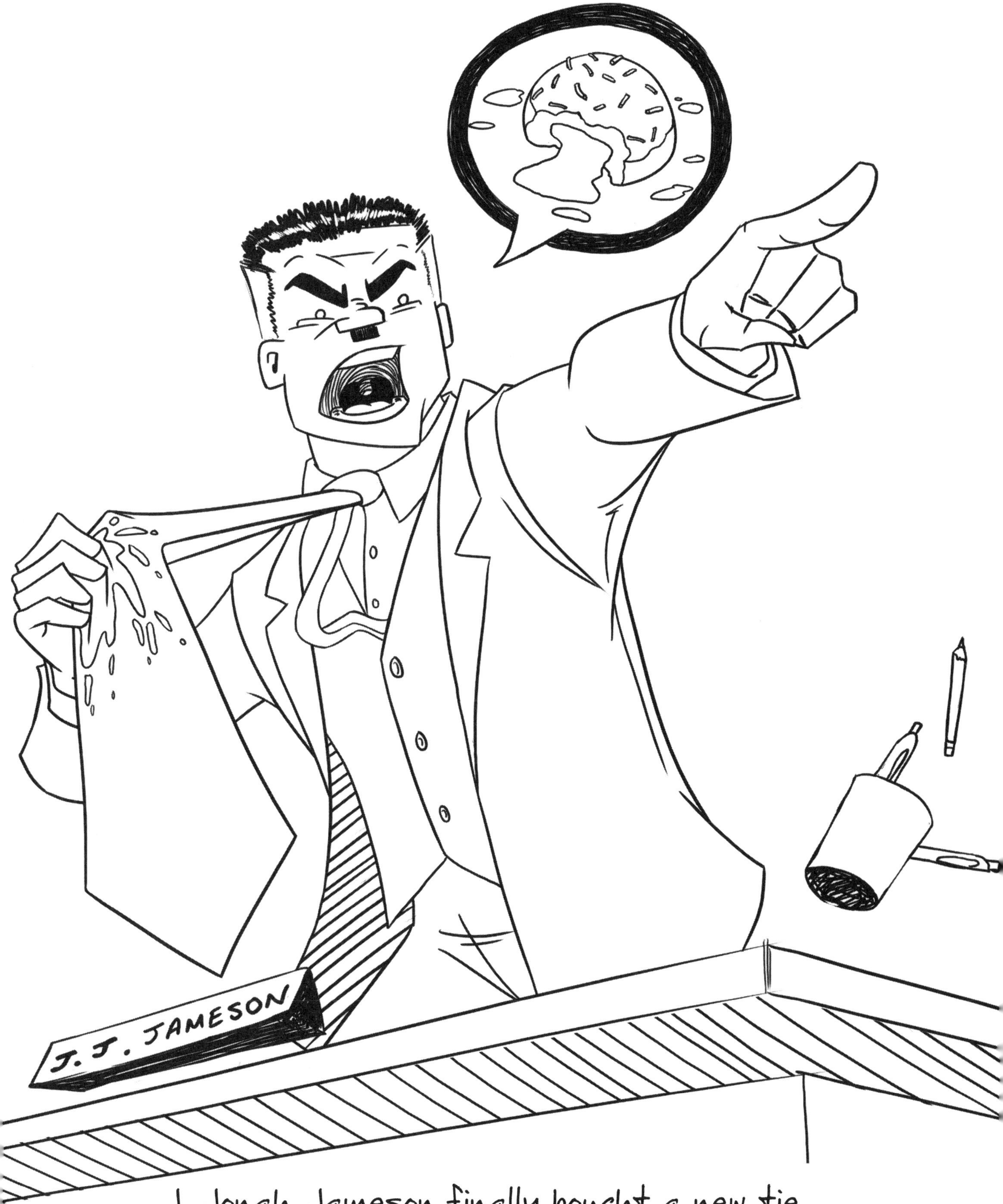
J. J. JAMESON

J. Jonah Jameson finally bought a new tie.
What does it look like?

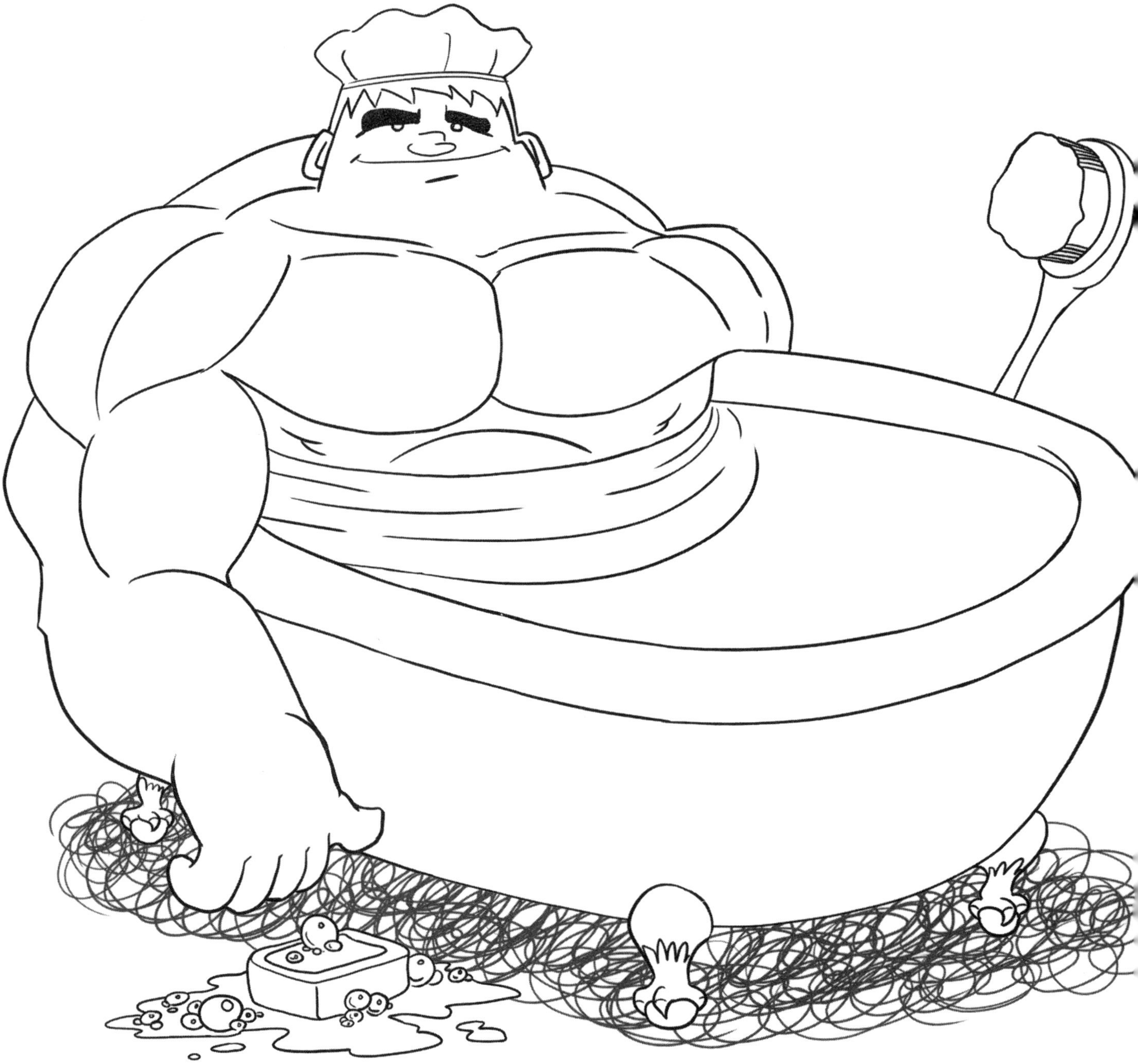

Hulk is taking a warm bath.
Draw some bubbles and maybe a rubber ducky.

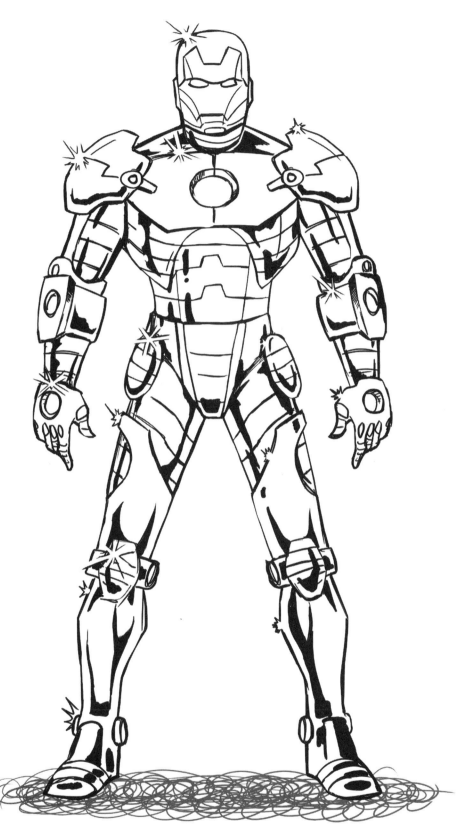

Give Iron Man some really cool
armor modifications.

Steve Rogers needs to get with the times.
Give him a new hairstyle.

Groot has taken up woodworking.
What did he build?

Drax has no sense of humor.
Go wild with doodles!

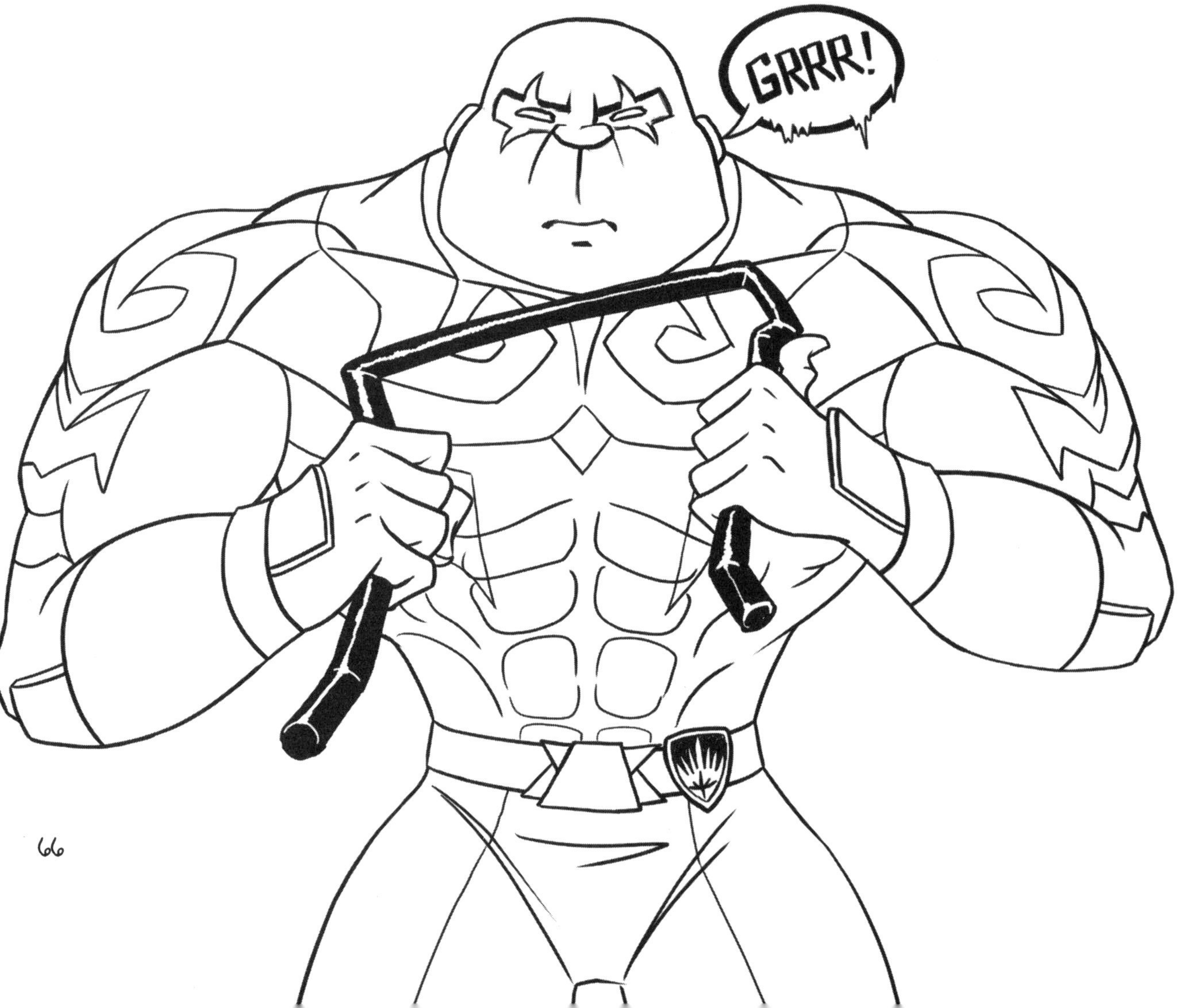
GRRR!

What did Gamora just cut in half?
Try not to be too gross.

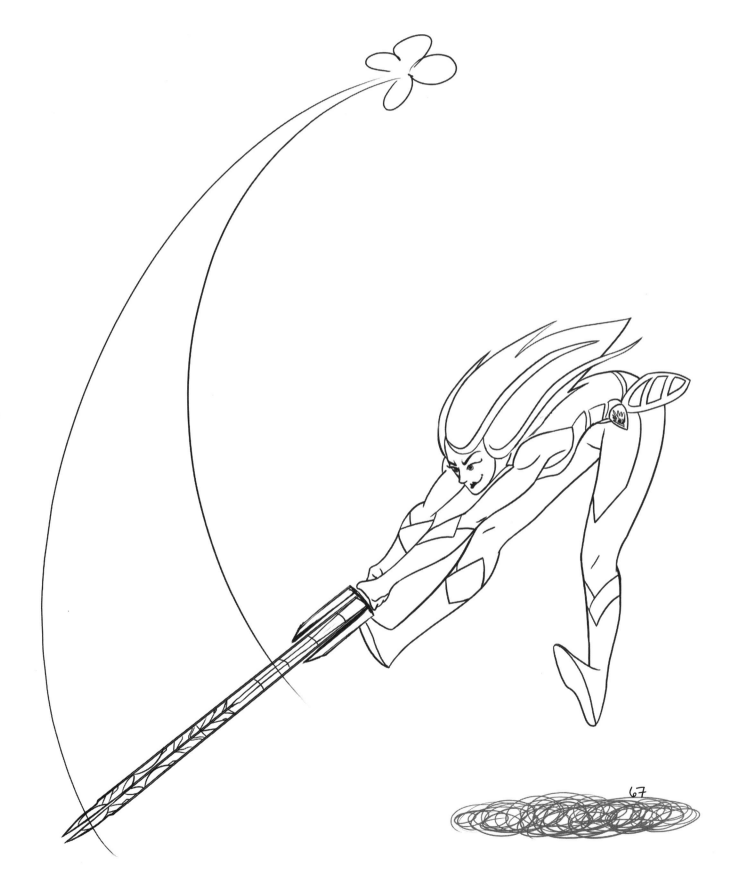

Nick Fury has crashed the
S.H.I.E.L.D. Helicarrier again.
Draw him a new one.

Look how tiny Ant-Man is! Draw lots of
tiny ants to keep him company.
How many can you draw?

Why is Hulk sad?

Help Red Skull build a new evil lair.
Don't make it very good.
He's a bad guy, remember!

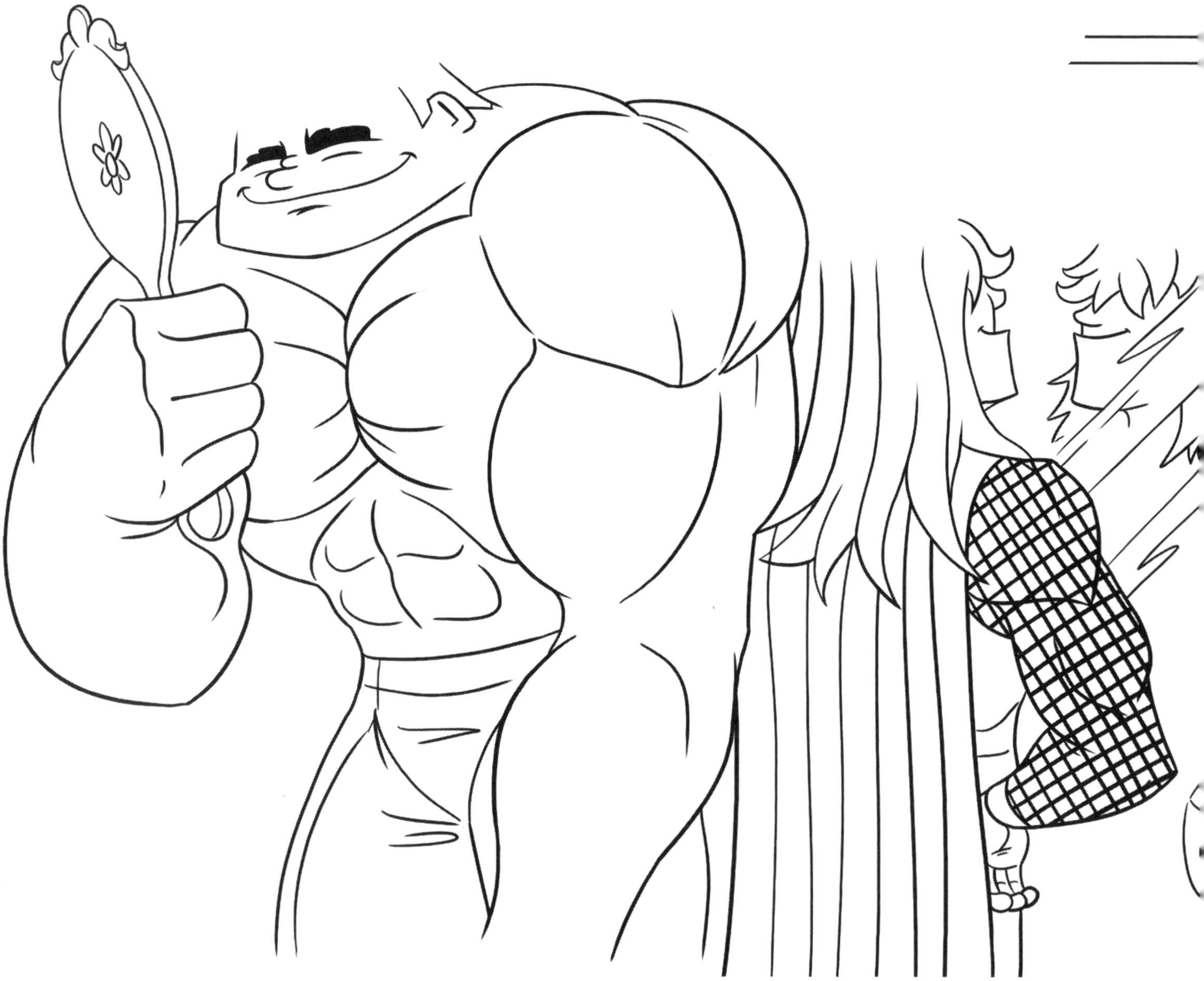

Hulk and Thor are trying on new hats.
What would look best on them?

Dress up these Chitauri invaders.
Make 'em look snazzy.

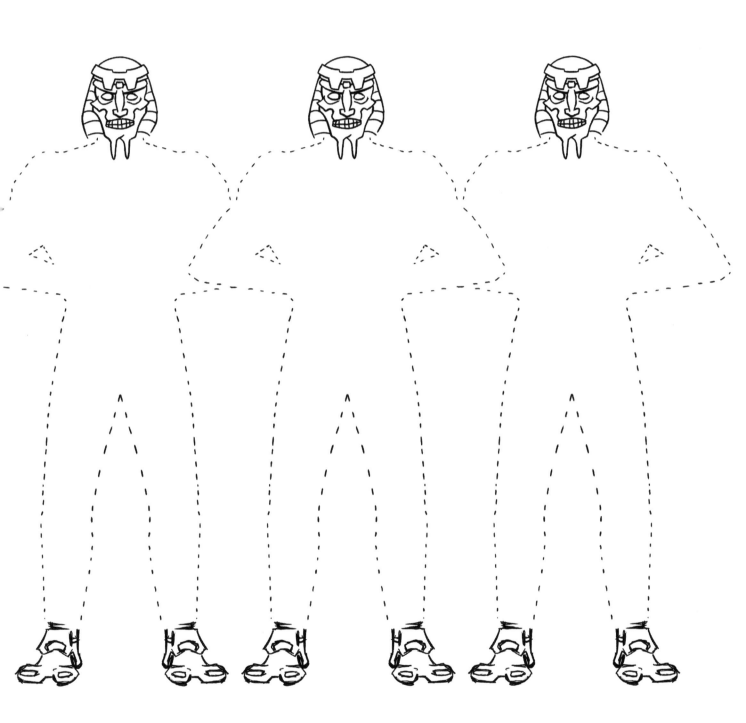

Draw Iron Man's repulsor fire. Maybe
some explosions, too!

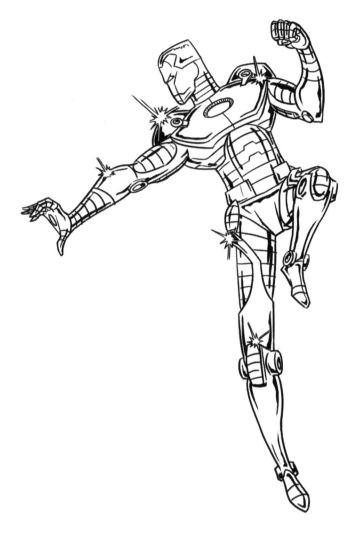

Luke Cage is sporting a new shirt.
Make it funky!

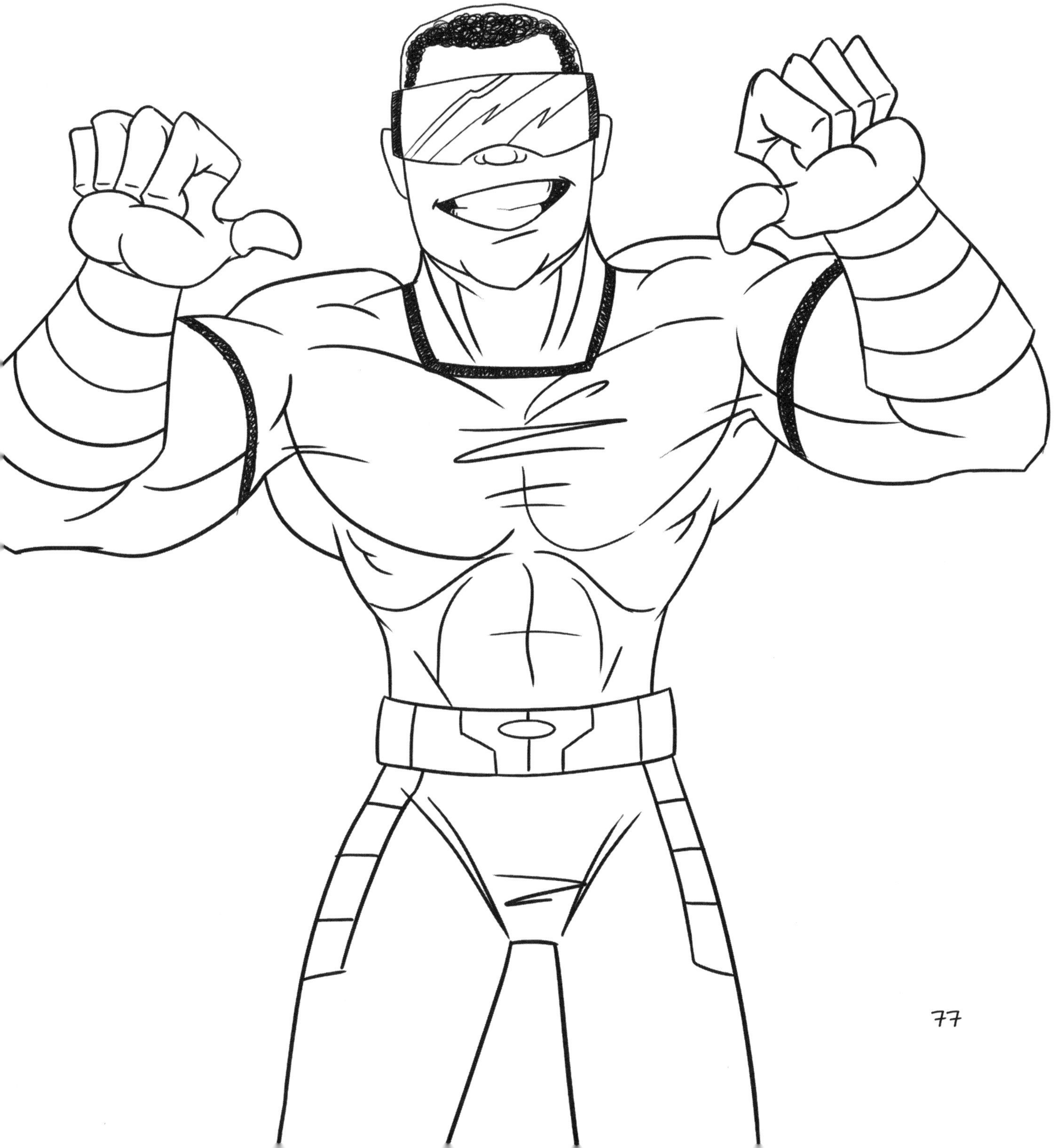

Ms. Marvel has stretchy arms.
Draw them.

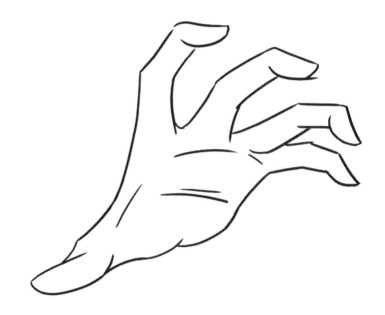

Spidey lost his mask.
Quick! Draw him a new one.

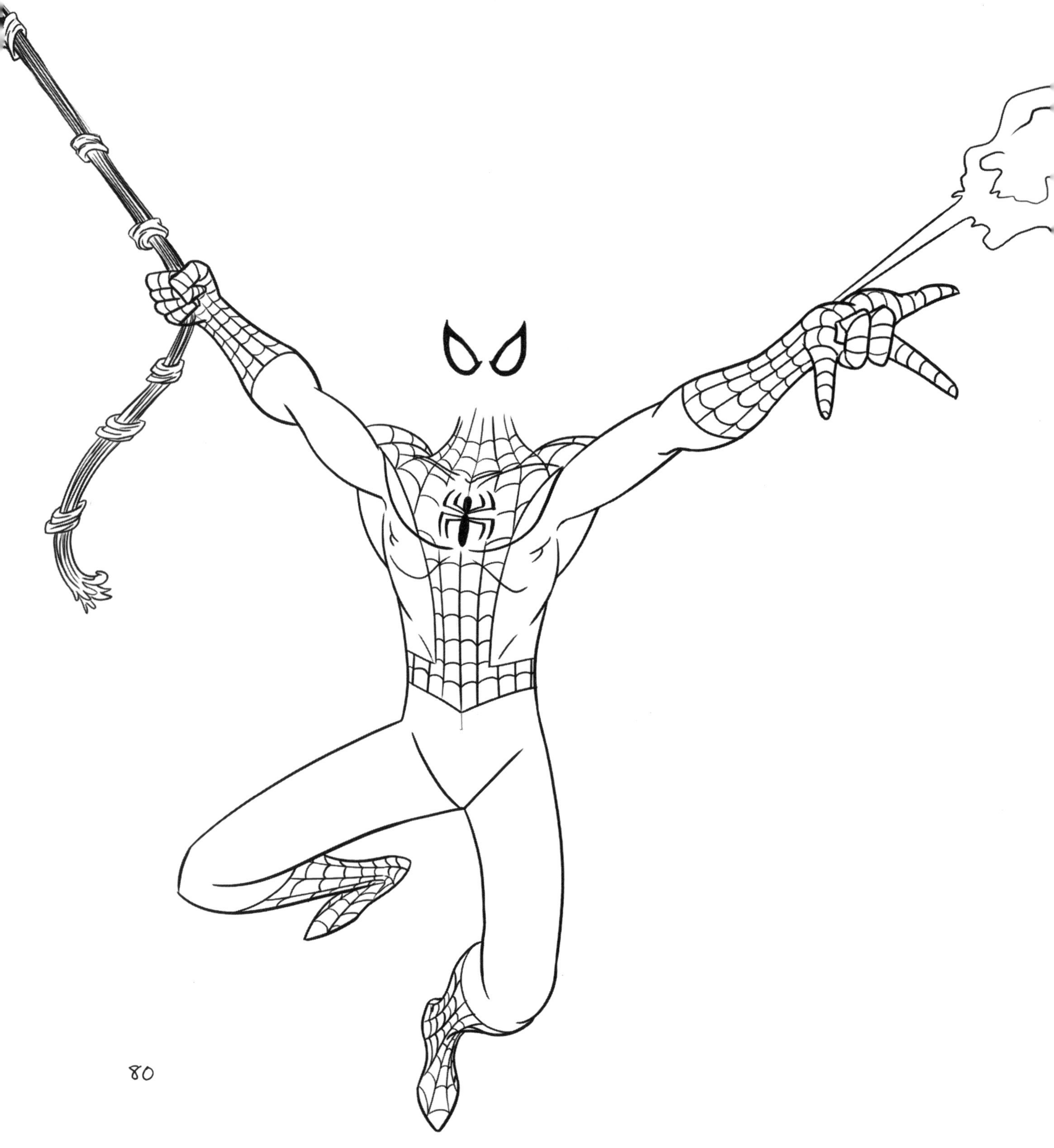

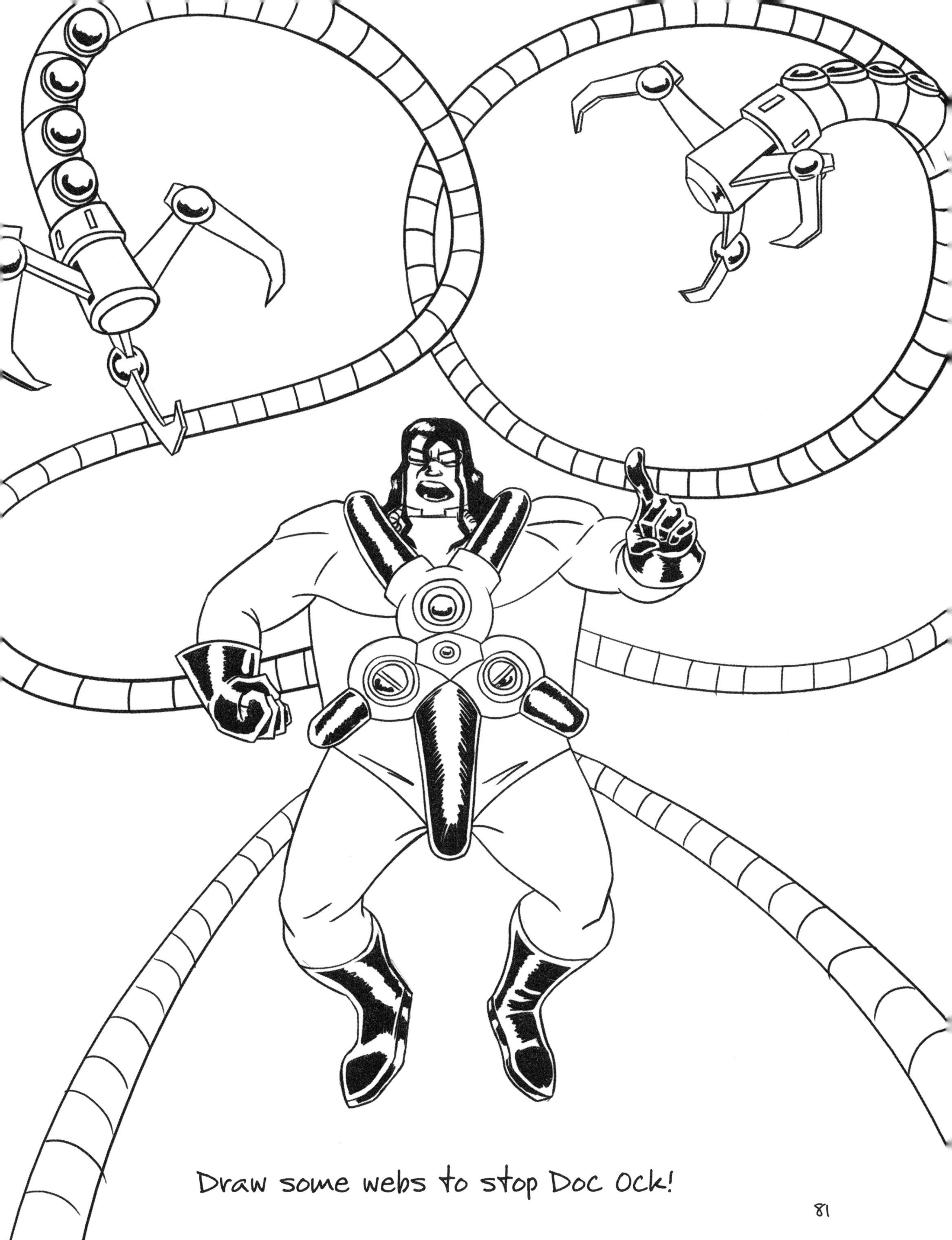

Draw some webs to stop Doc Ock!

Draw stars and explosions to help the Avengers defeat Ultron.

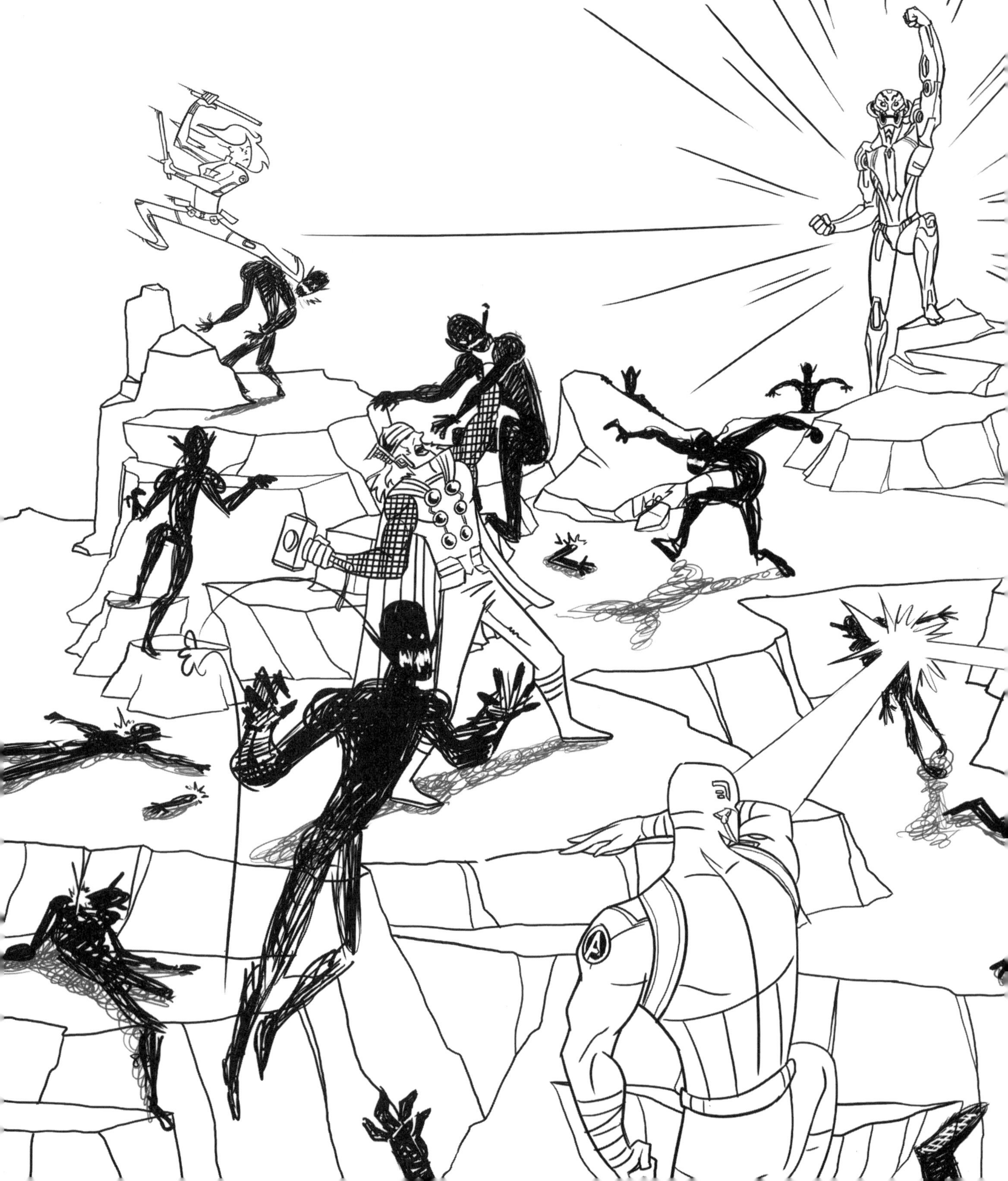

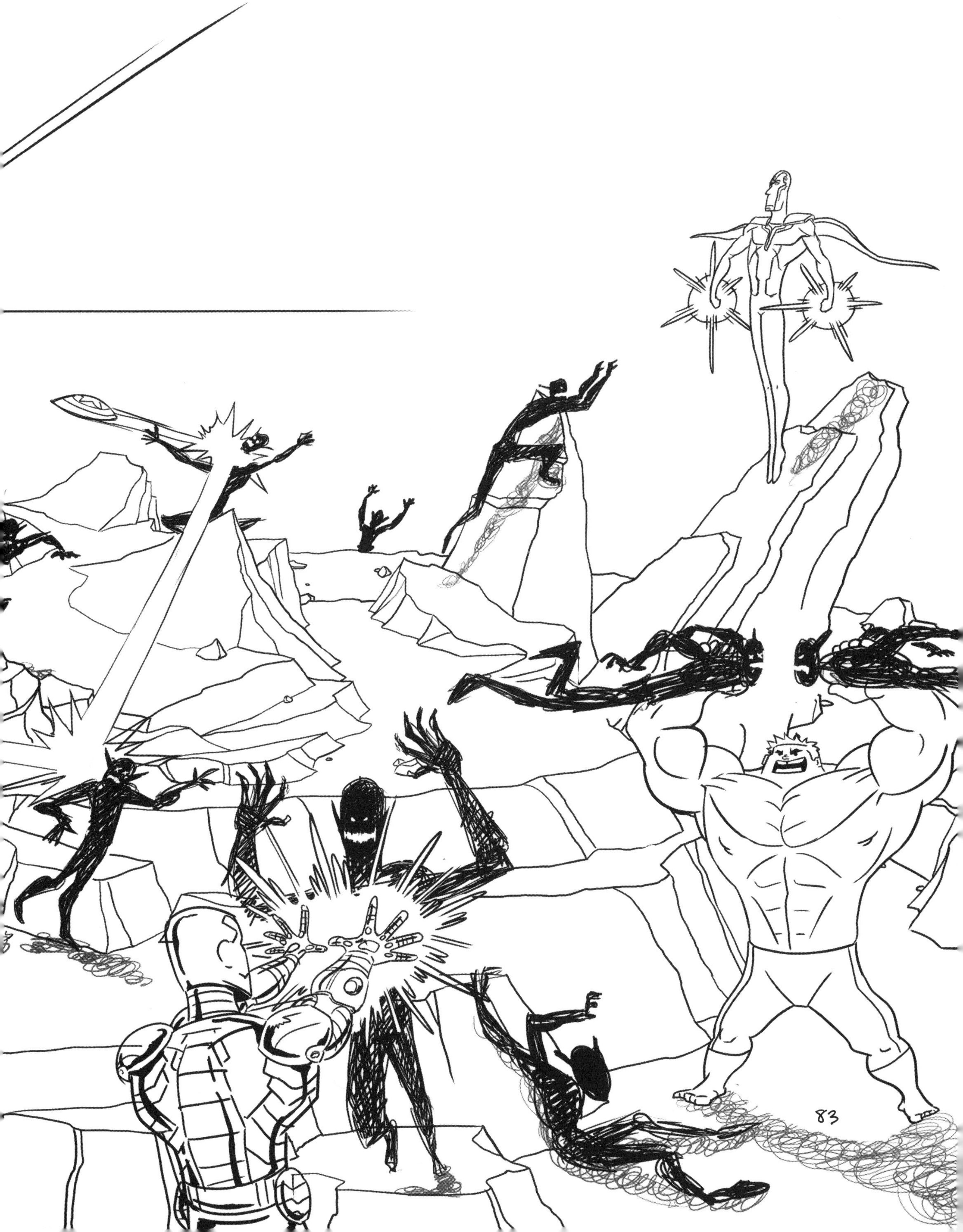

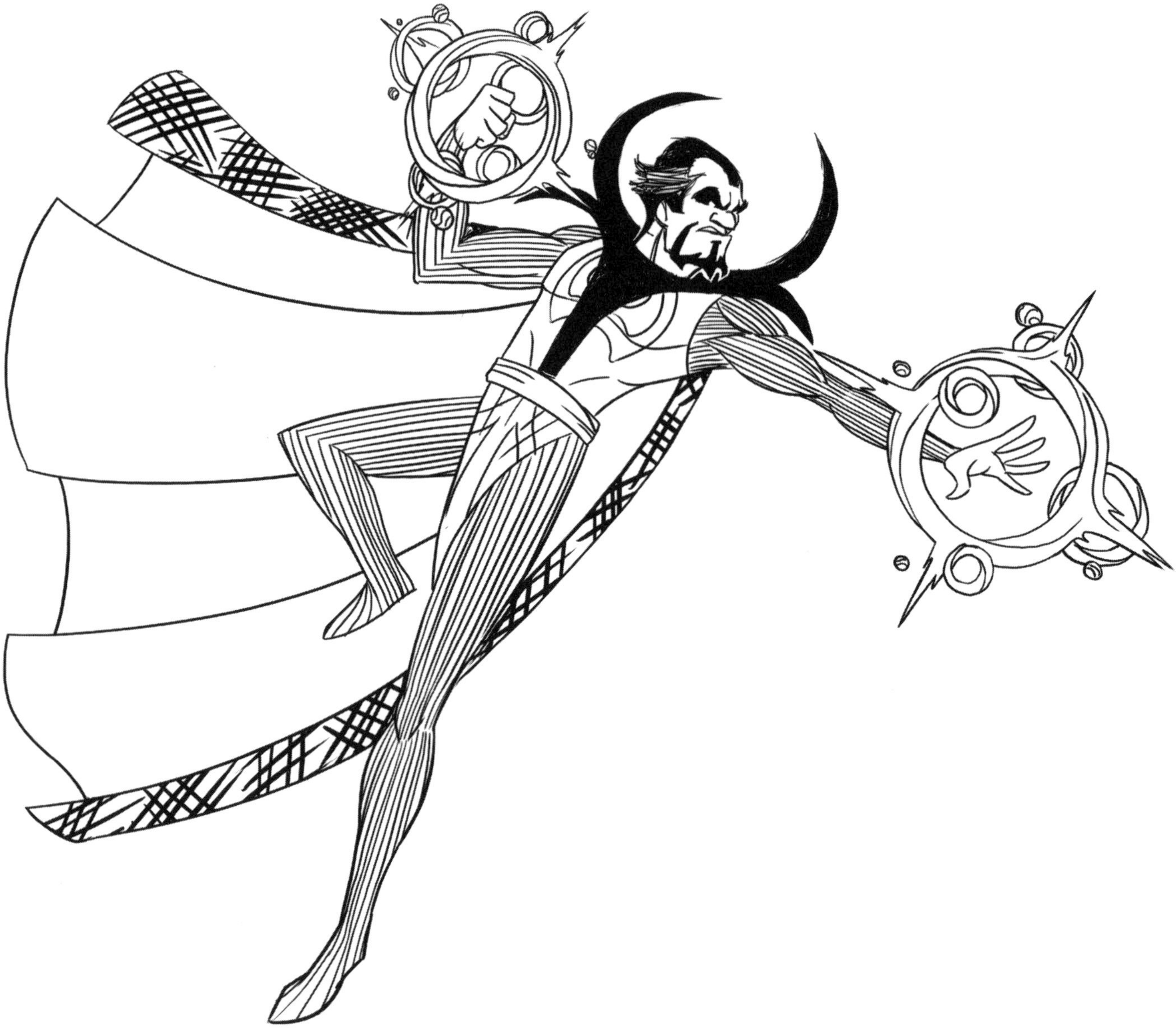

Draw some magic to help Doctor Strange defeat Baron Mordo.

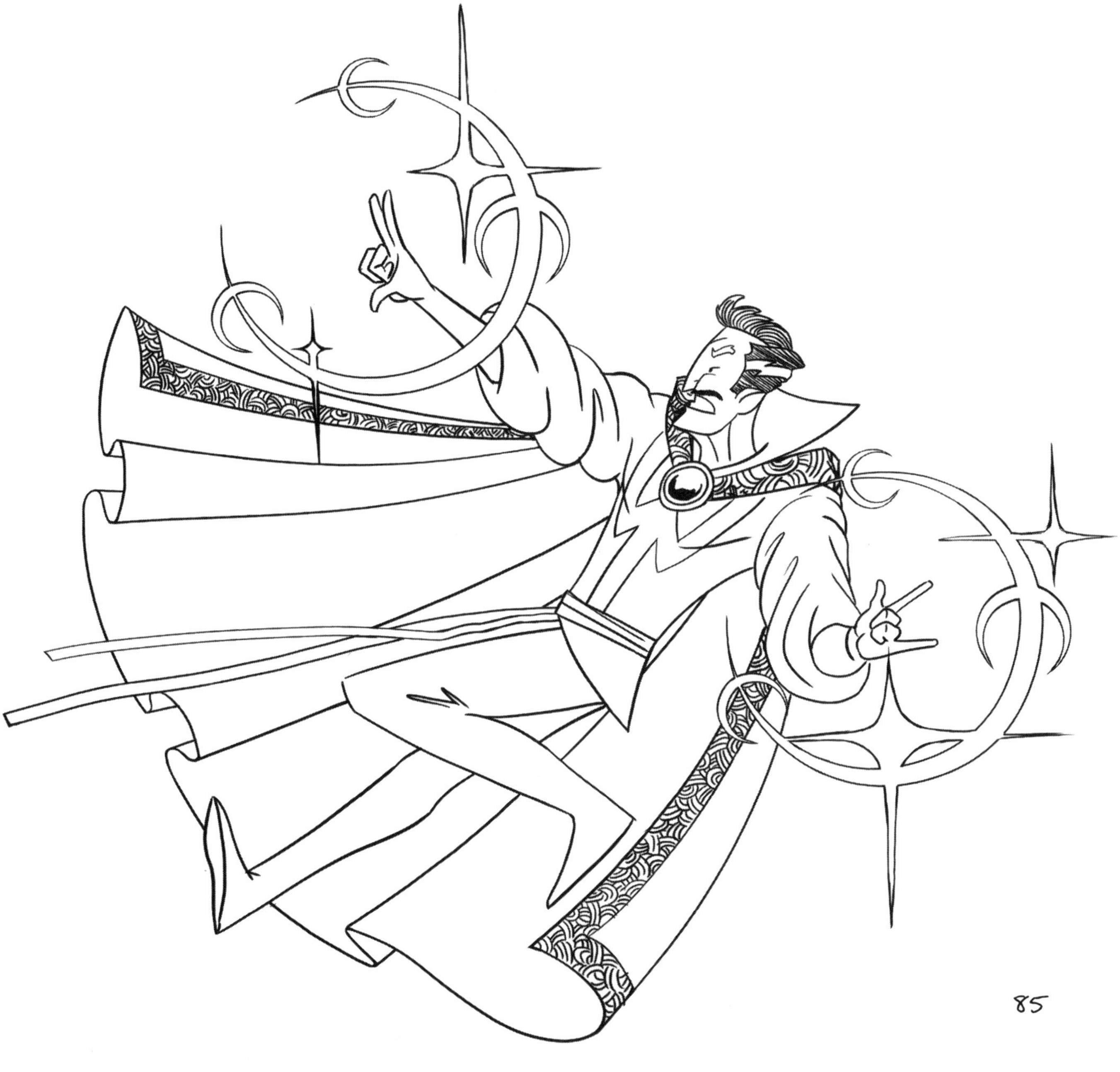

What is Black Panther jumping over?

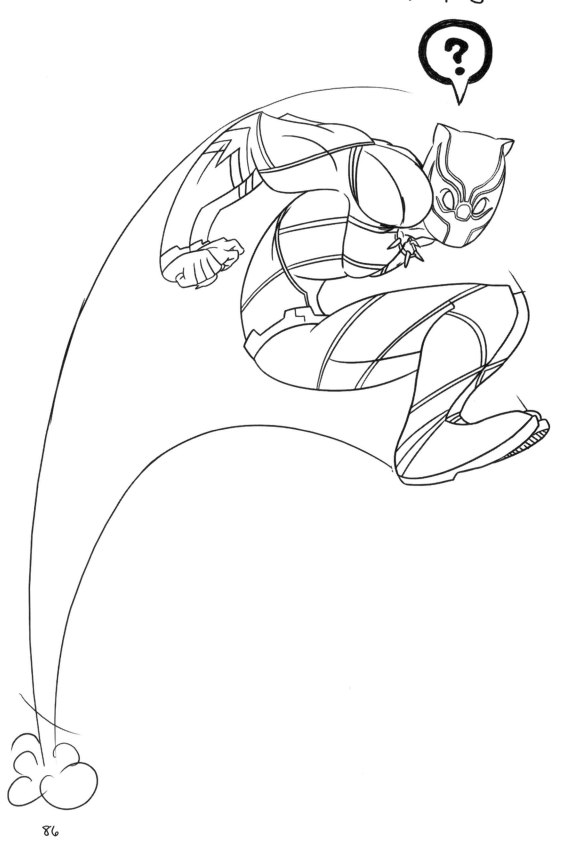

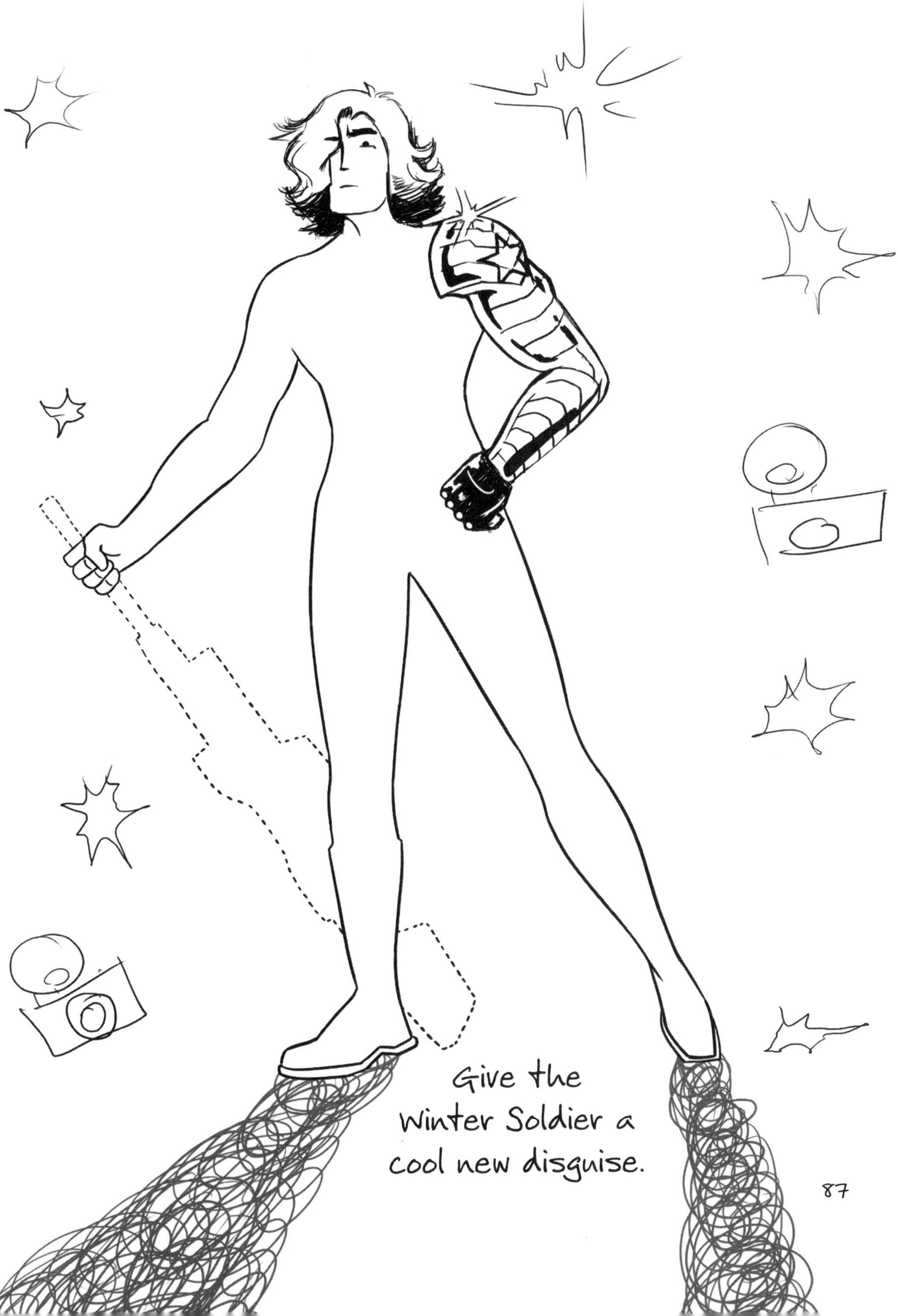

Give the
Winter Soldier a
cool new disguise.

Draw zigzags to show the lightning coming from Thor's hammer.

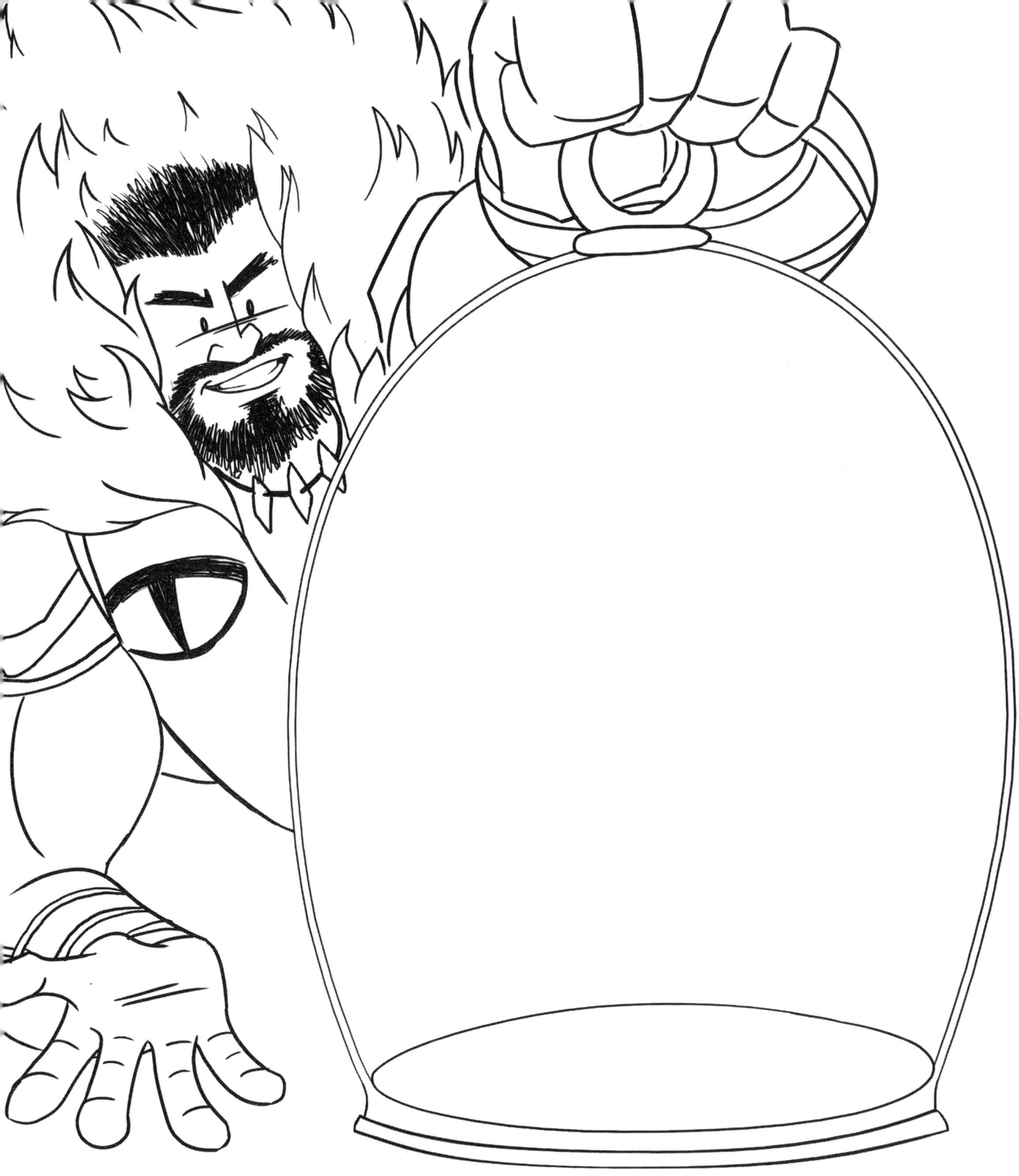

Kraven caught something in his cage trap.
What is it?

Draw POWS! and stars to help the Guardians of the Galaxy defeat the Chitauri invaders.

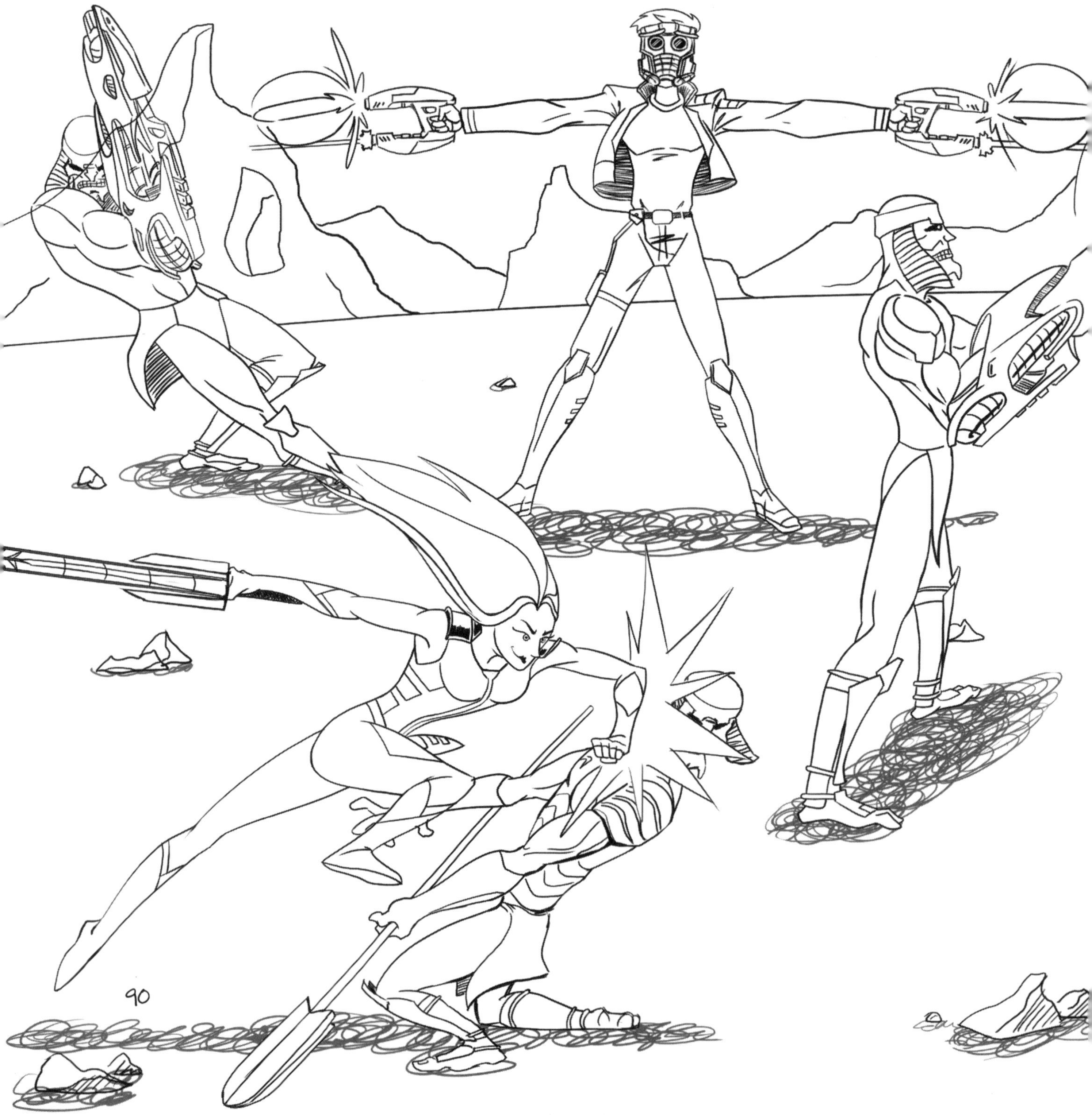

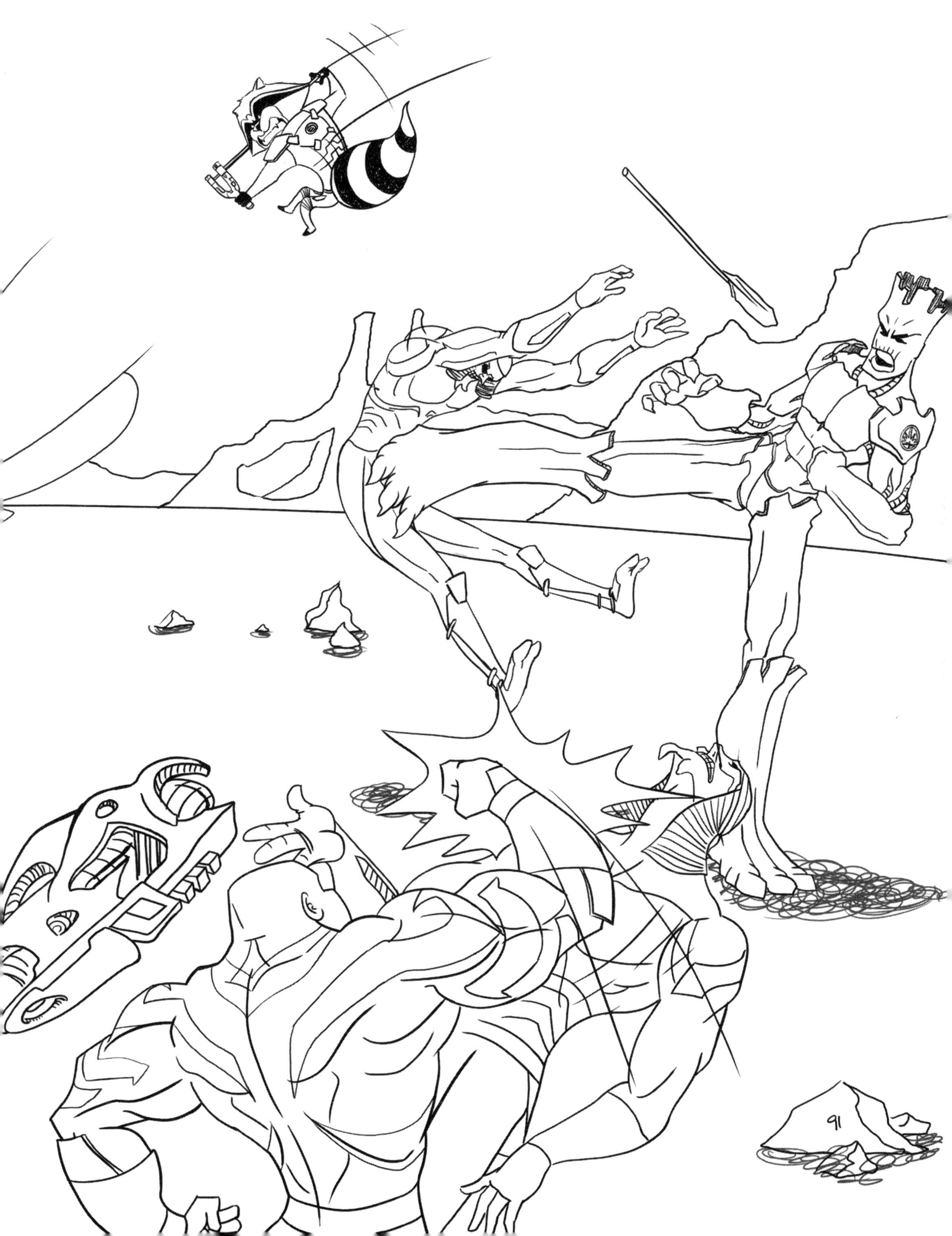

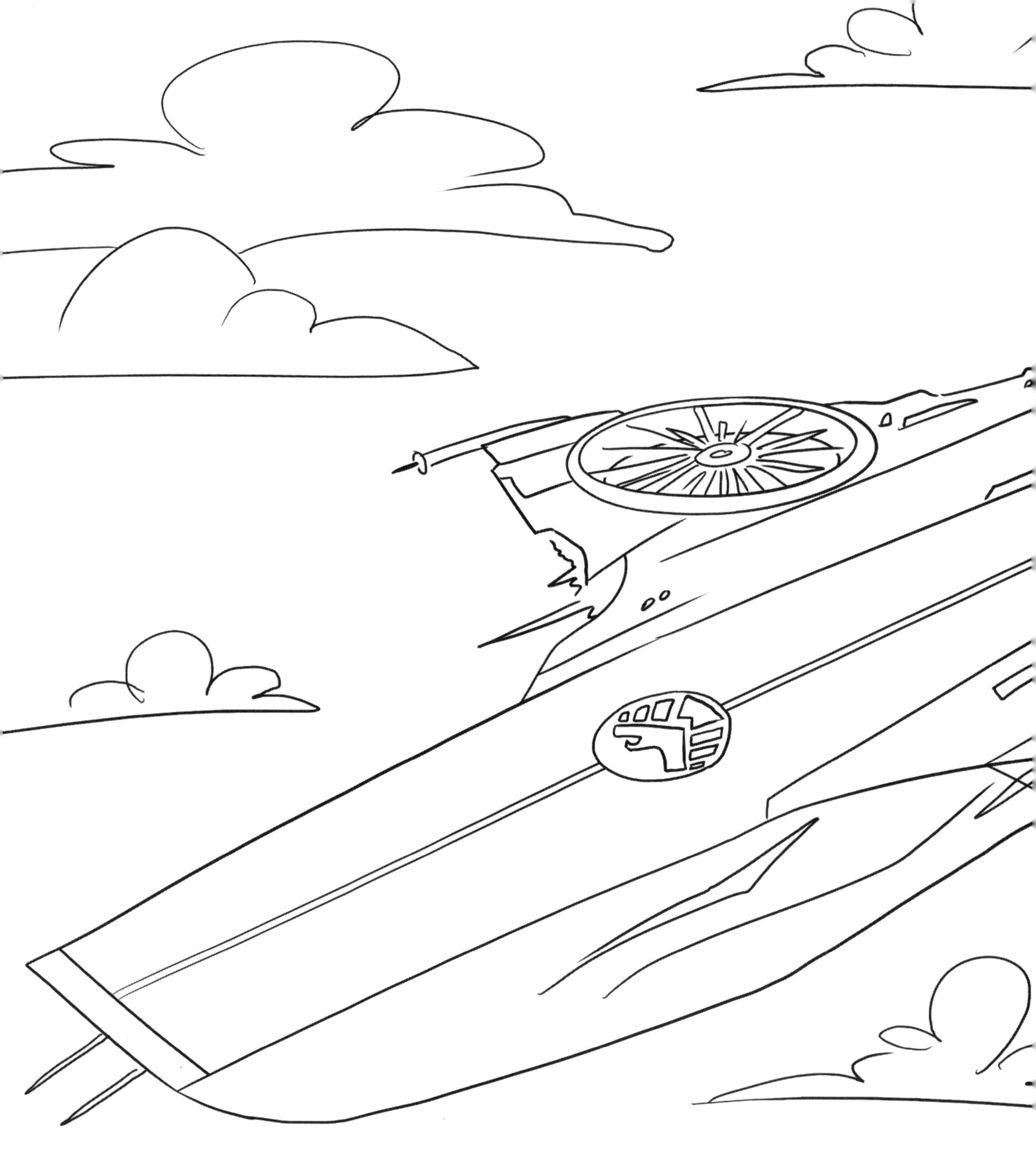

The S.H.I.E.L.D. Helicarrier needs a swimming pool. Draw one, or whatever else you think it needs to increase its resale value.

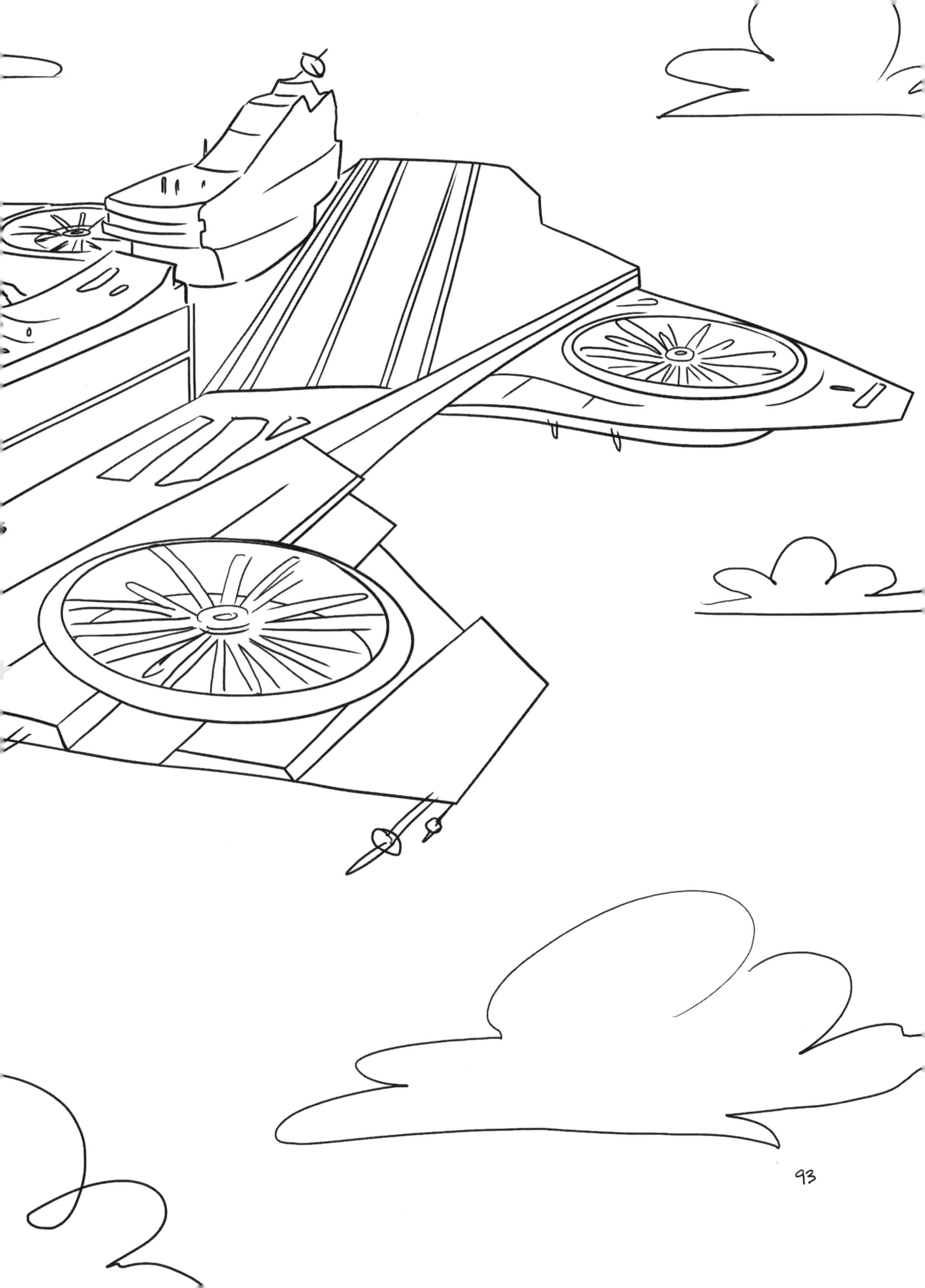

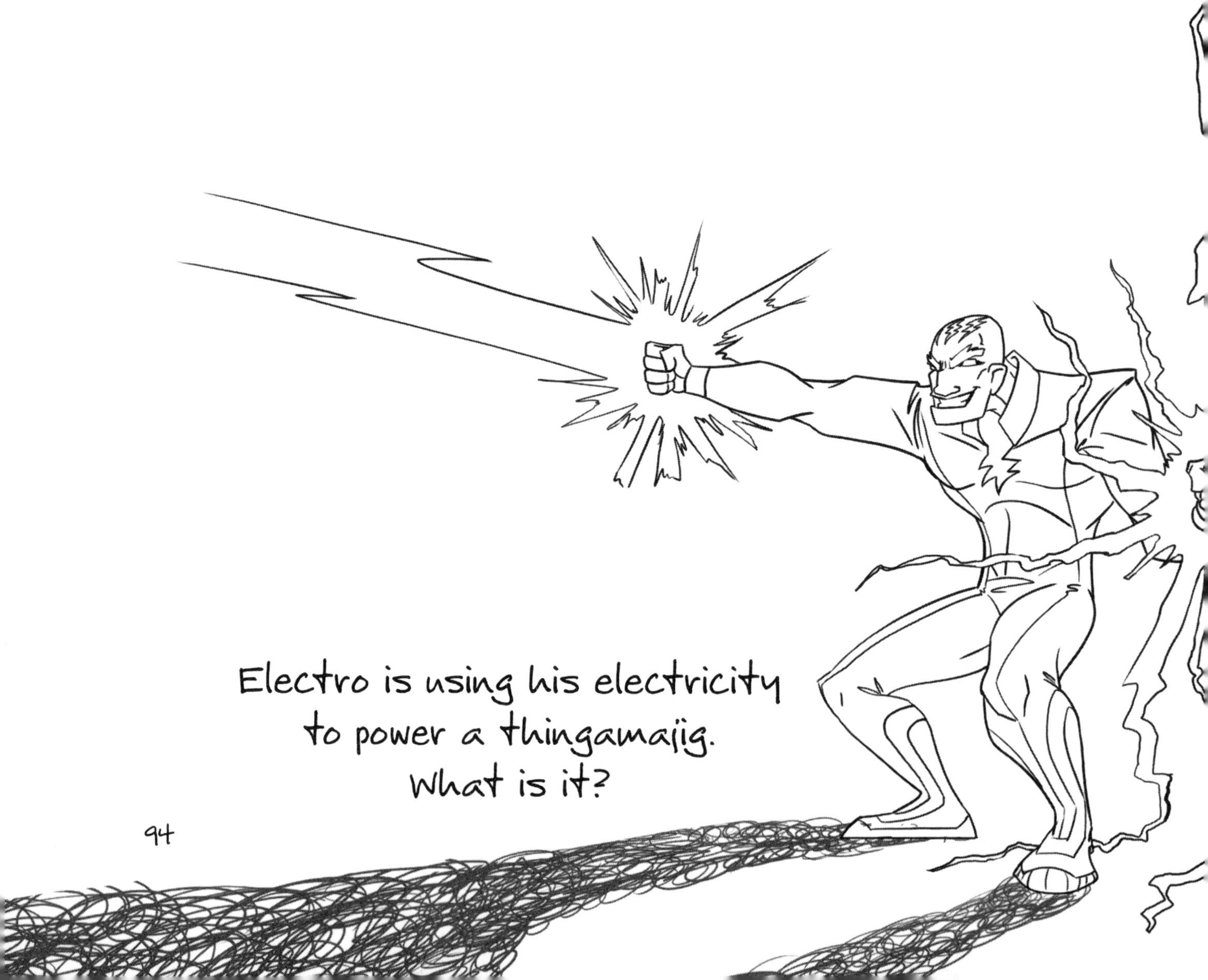

Electro is using his electricity
to power a thingamajig.
What is it?

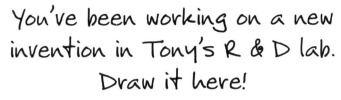

You've been working on a new
invention in Tony's R & D lab.
Draw it here!

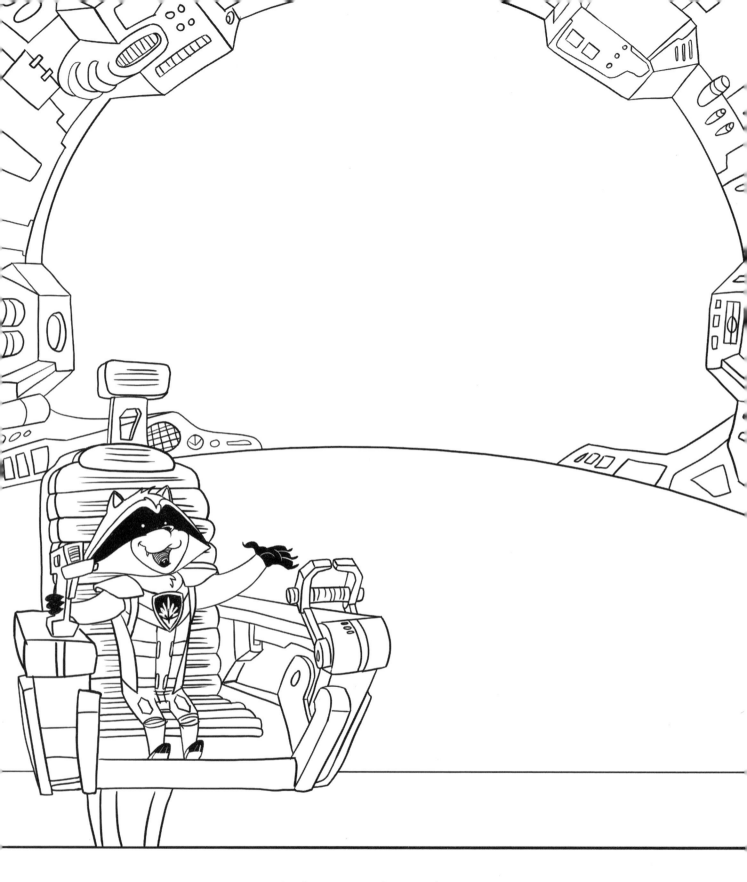

Rocket is piloting the Milano.
What do the controls look like?

Ant-Man is flying on a creepy-crawly bug.
What does it look like?

Hint: it has twelve eyes!

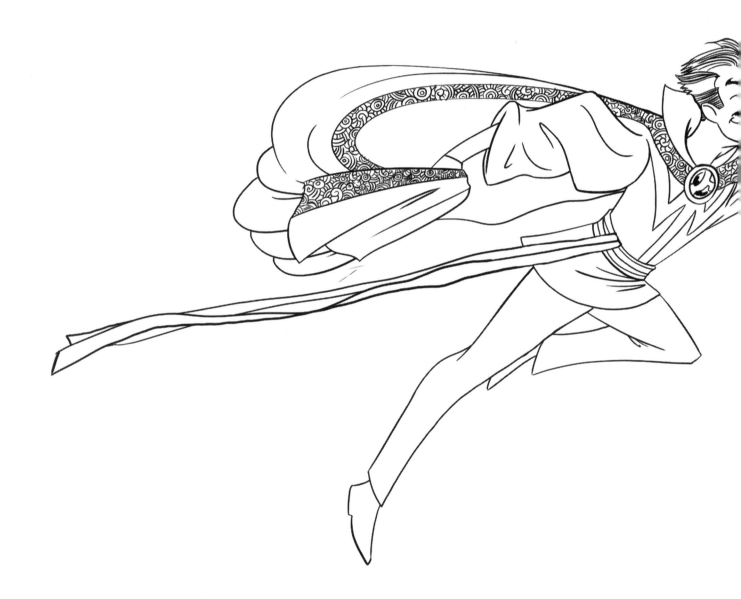

Doctor Strange is flying through another dimension.
What does it look like? Who lives there?

Spider-Man, Ant-Man, and Black Widow just came up with a cool Super Hero name.
Draw the logo here!

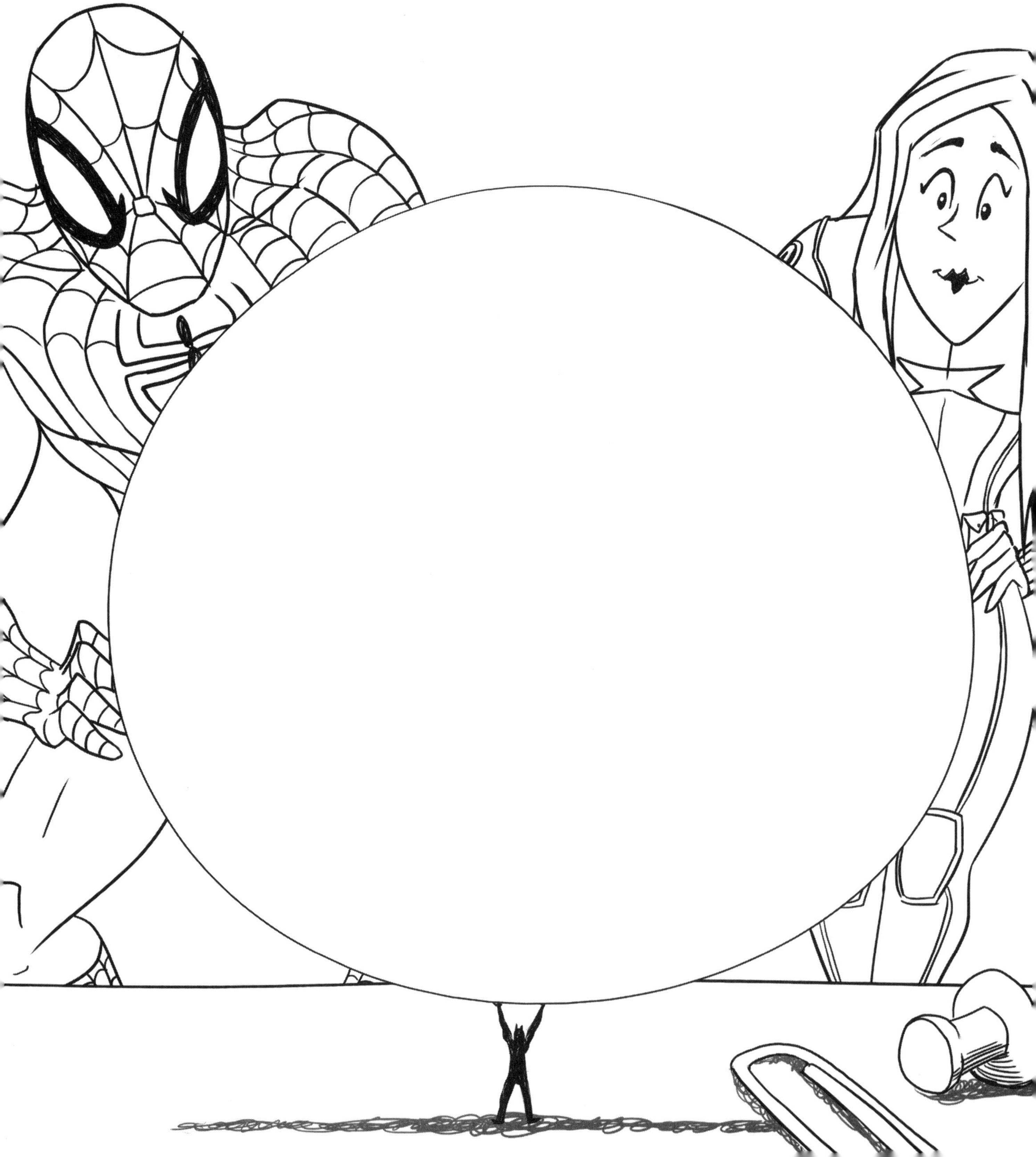

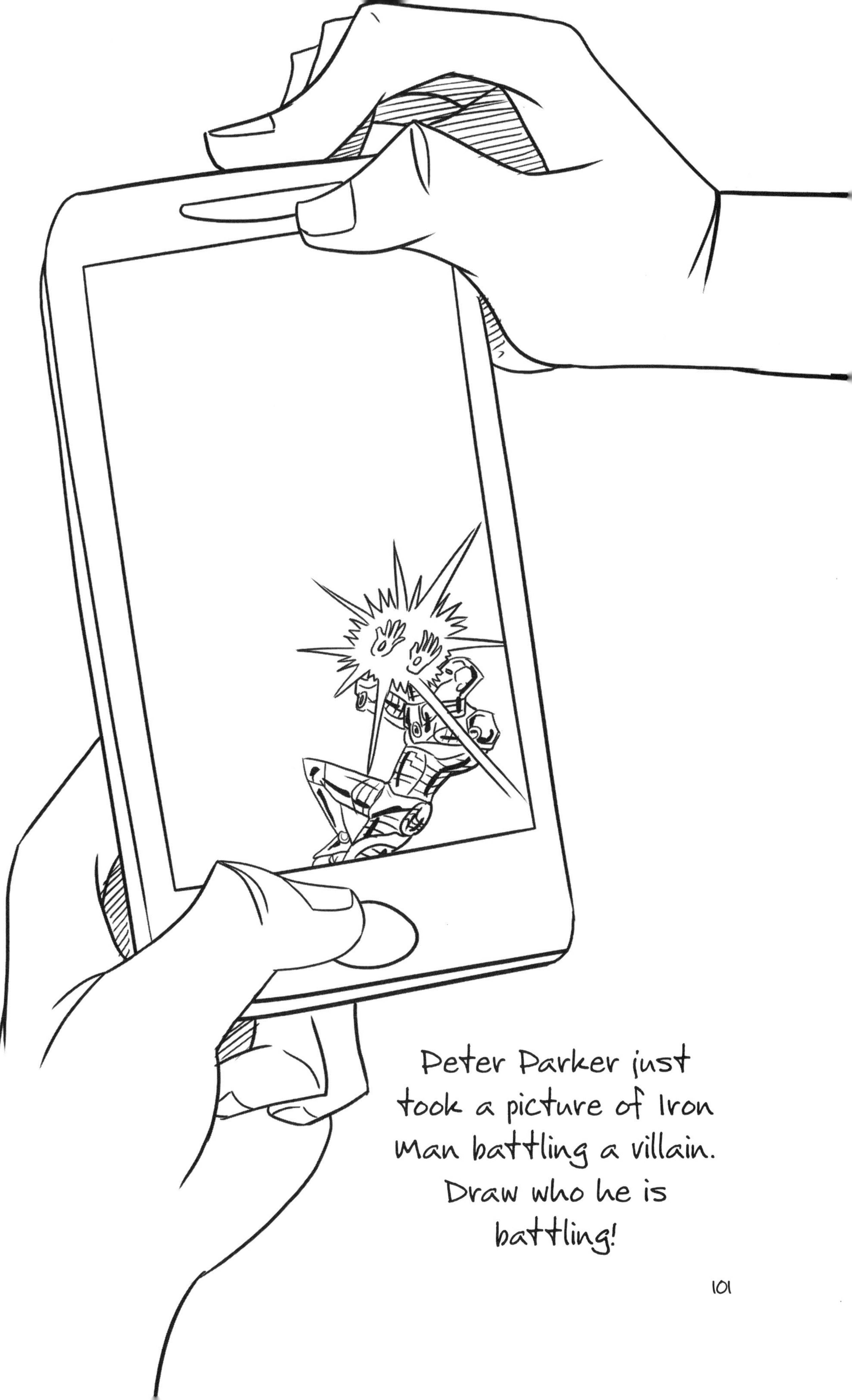

Peter Parker just took a picture of Iron Man battling a villain. Draw who he is battling!

The Guardians of the Galaxy are on vacation!
Where did they go?

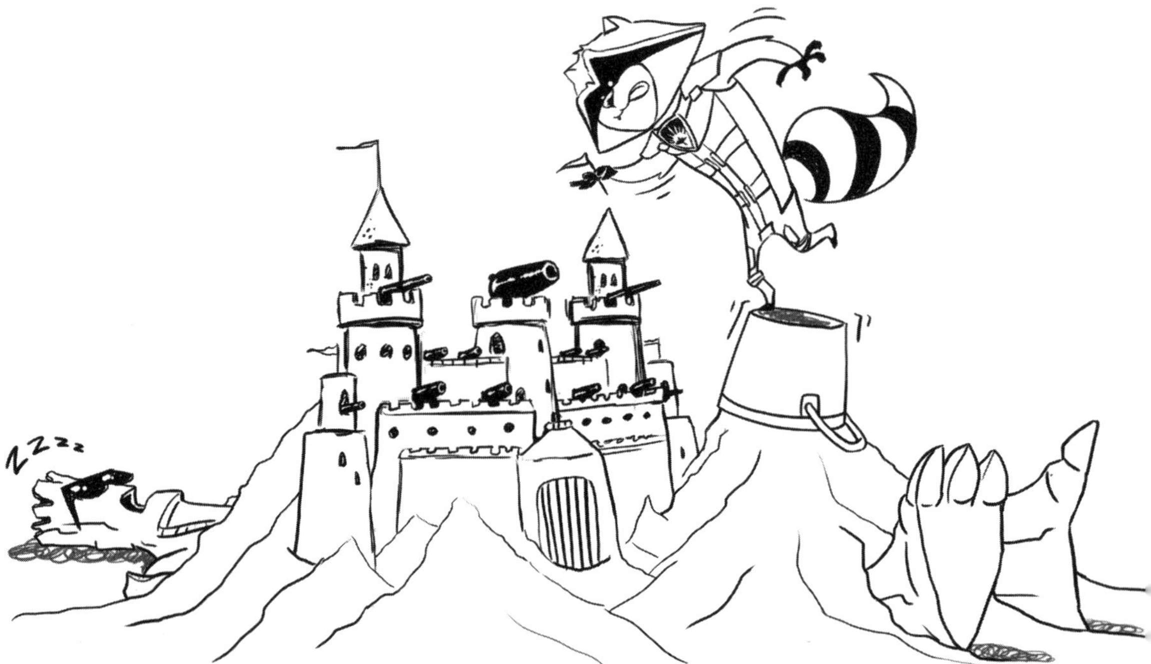
ZZZzz

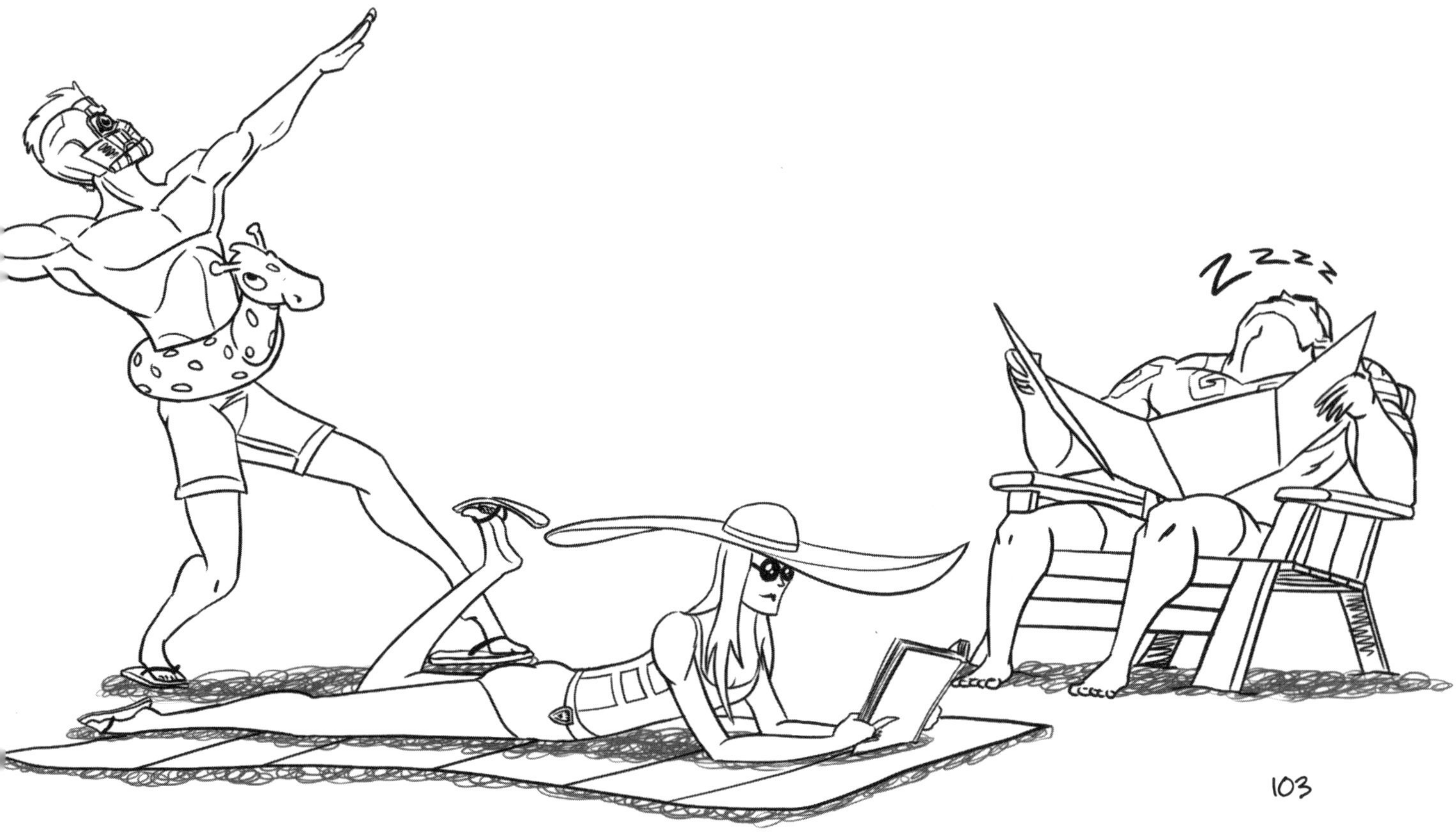
Zzzz

What's the first thing that pops in your head
when you think of Thor?
Draw it in sixty seconds!

What are Ant-Man and Spider-Man talking about?
Draw some speech bubbles.

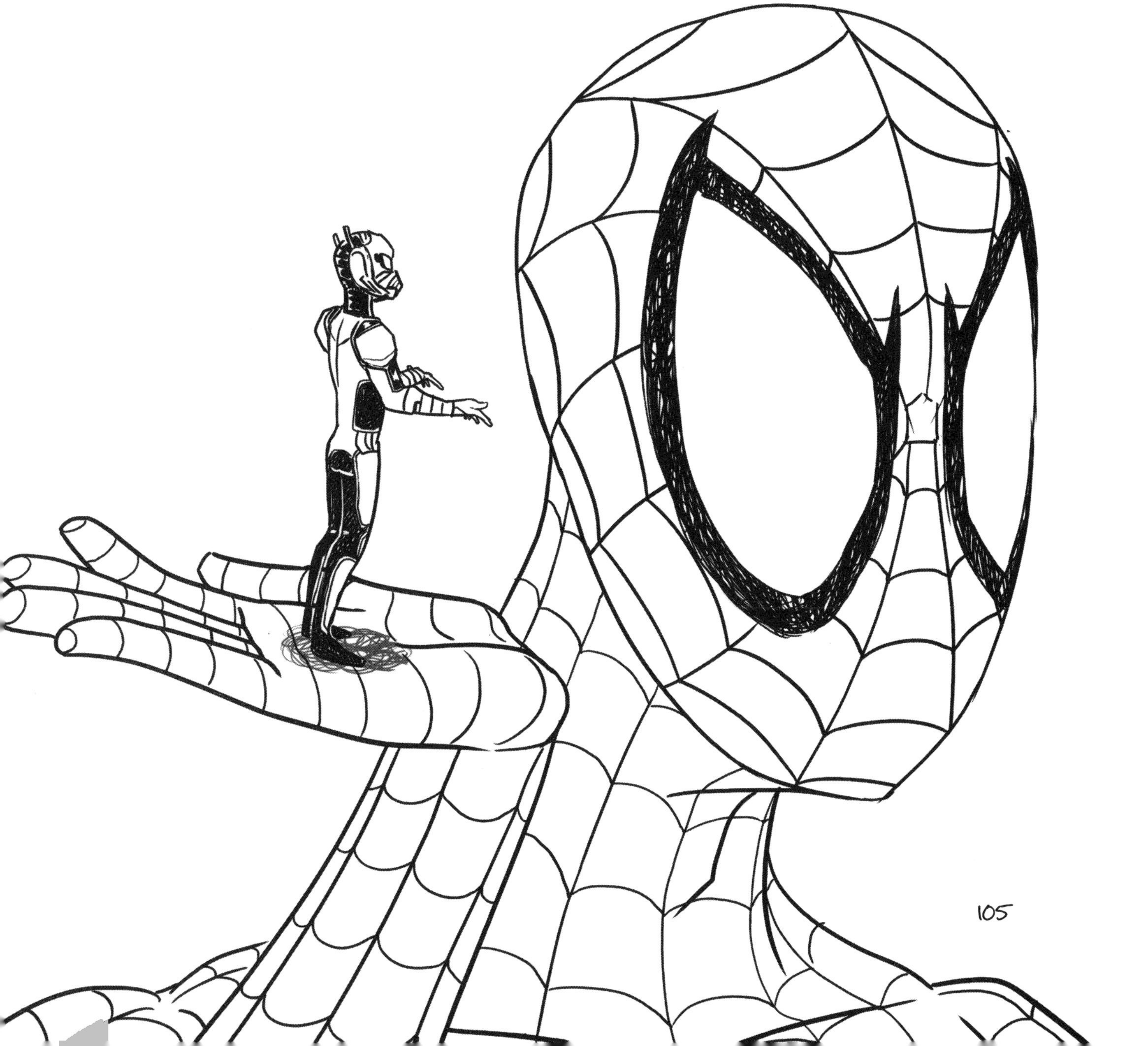

The Avengers need a new base.
Draw what it should look like!

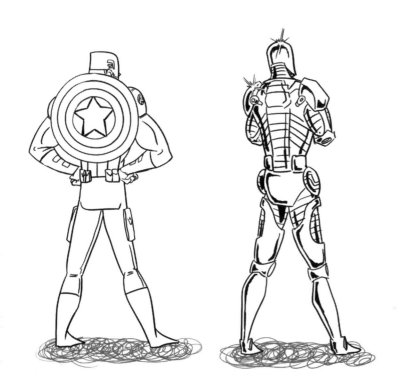

Loki is taking a painting class.
What has he painted on his canvas?

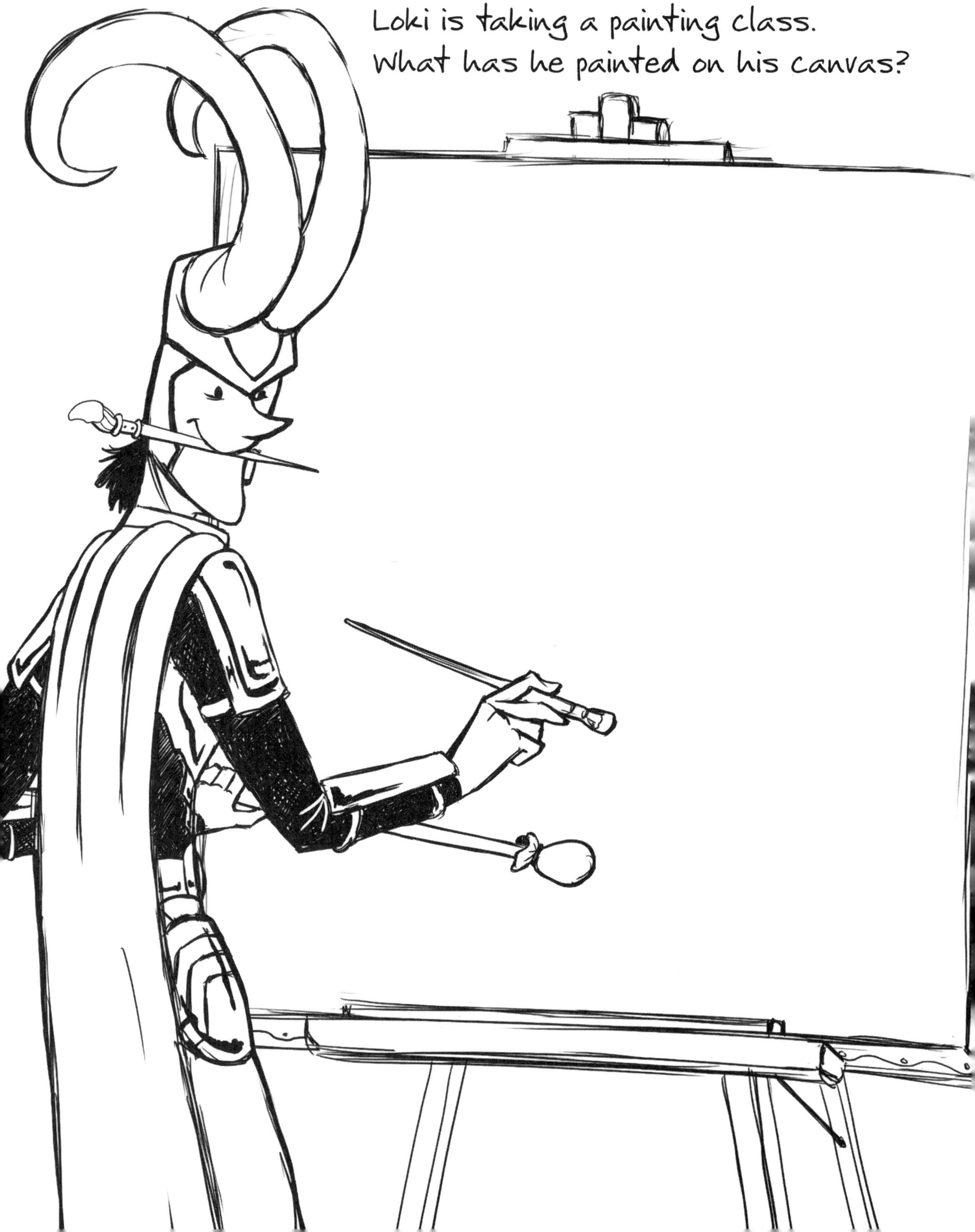

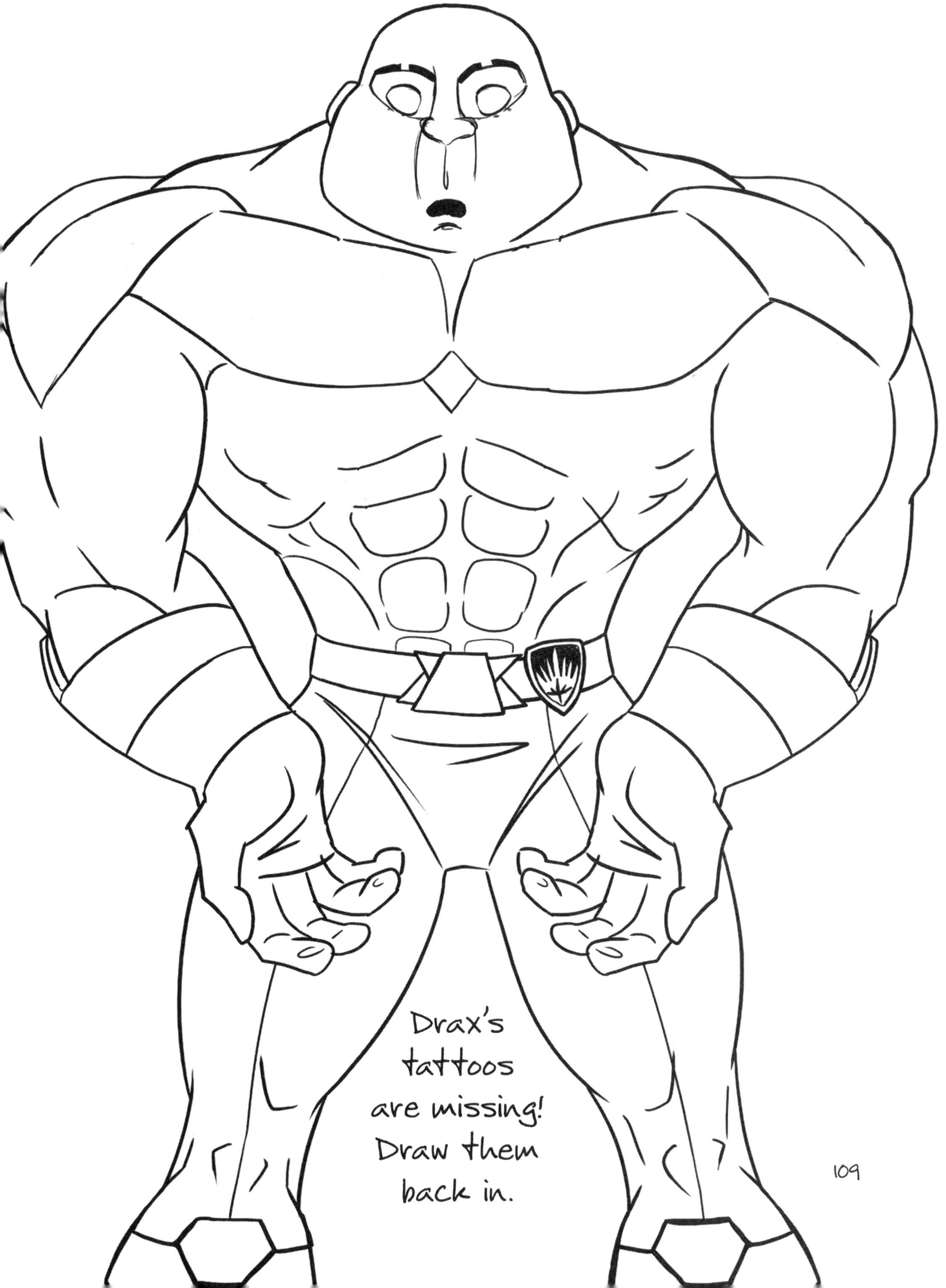

Drax's tattoos are missing! Draw them back in.

Spidey is after a new villain!
Draw the baddie's face on the poster to help
Spider-Man find him or her.

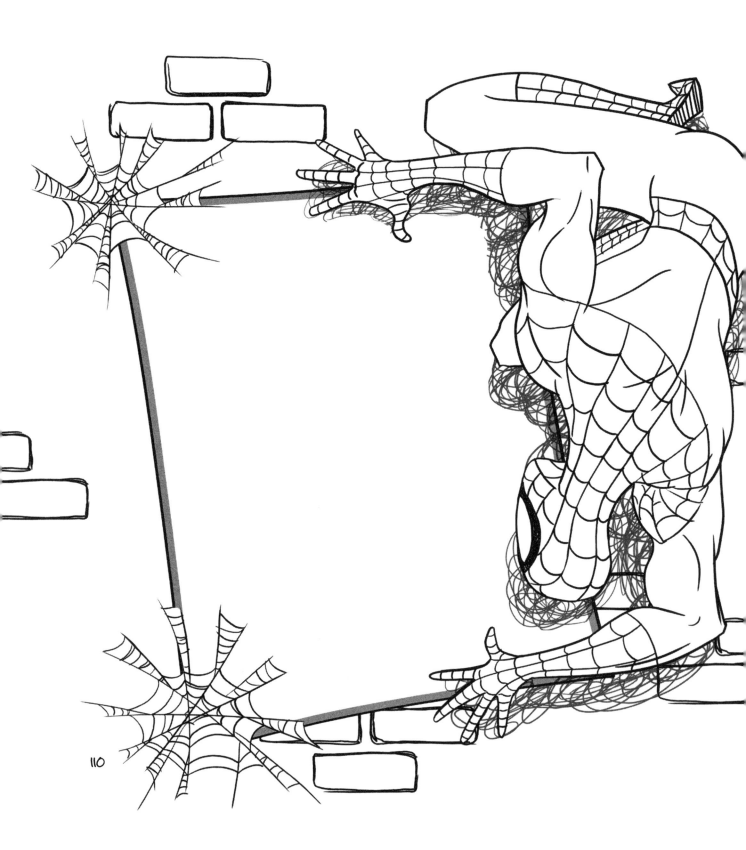

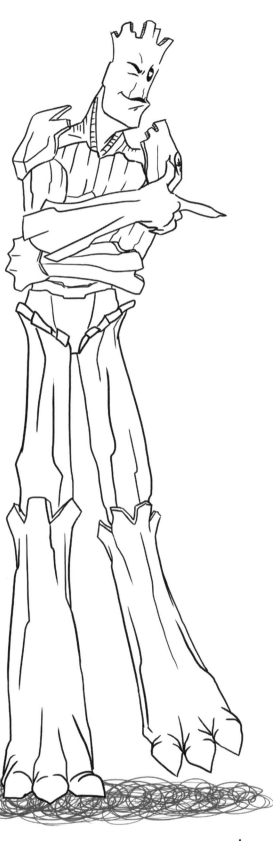

Groot says only "I AM GROOT."
If you could say only one thing, what would it be?
Draw yourself and your favorite line!

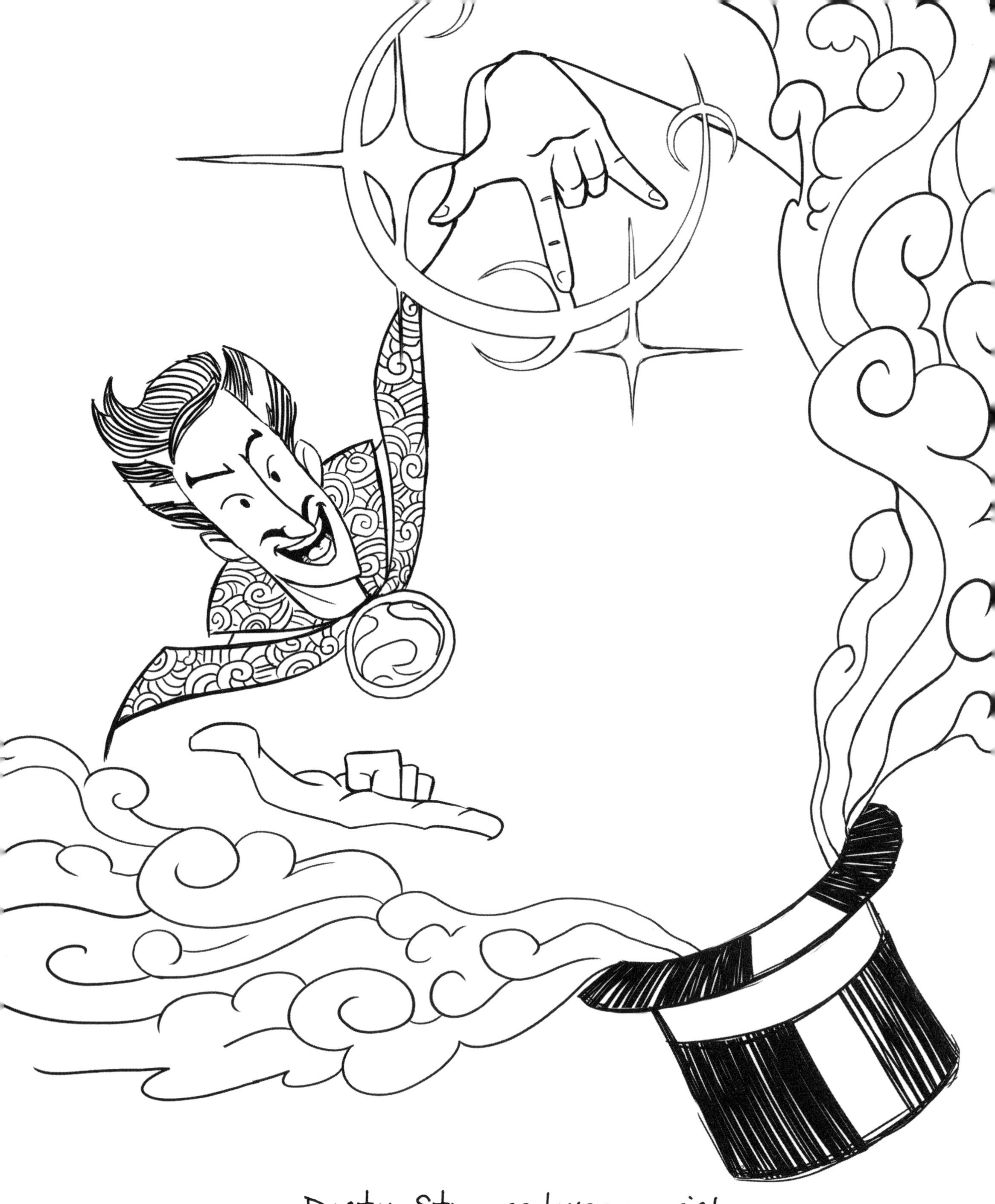

Doctor Strange loves magic!
Draw a rabbit coming out of the big top hat!

Tony just bought a brand-new boat for
himself and his fellow Avengers.
What does it look like?

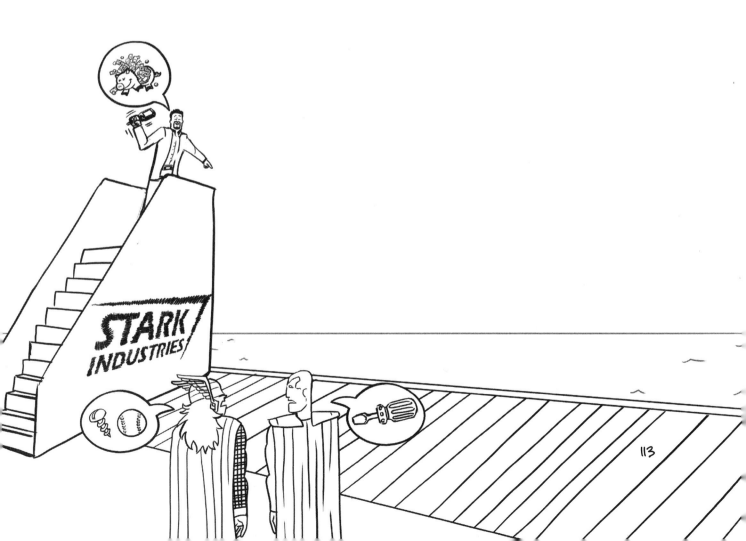

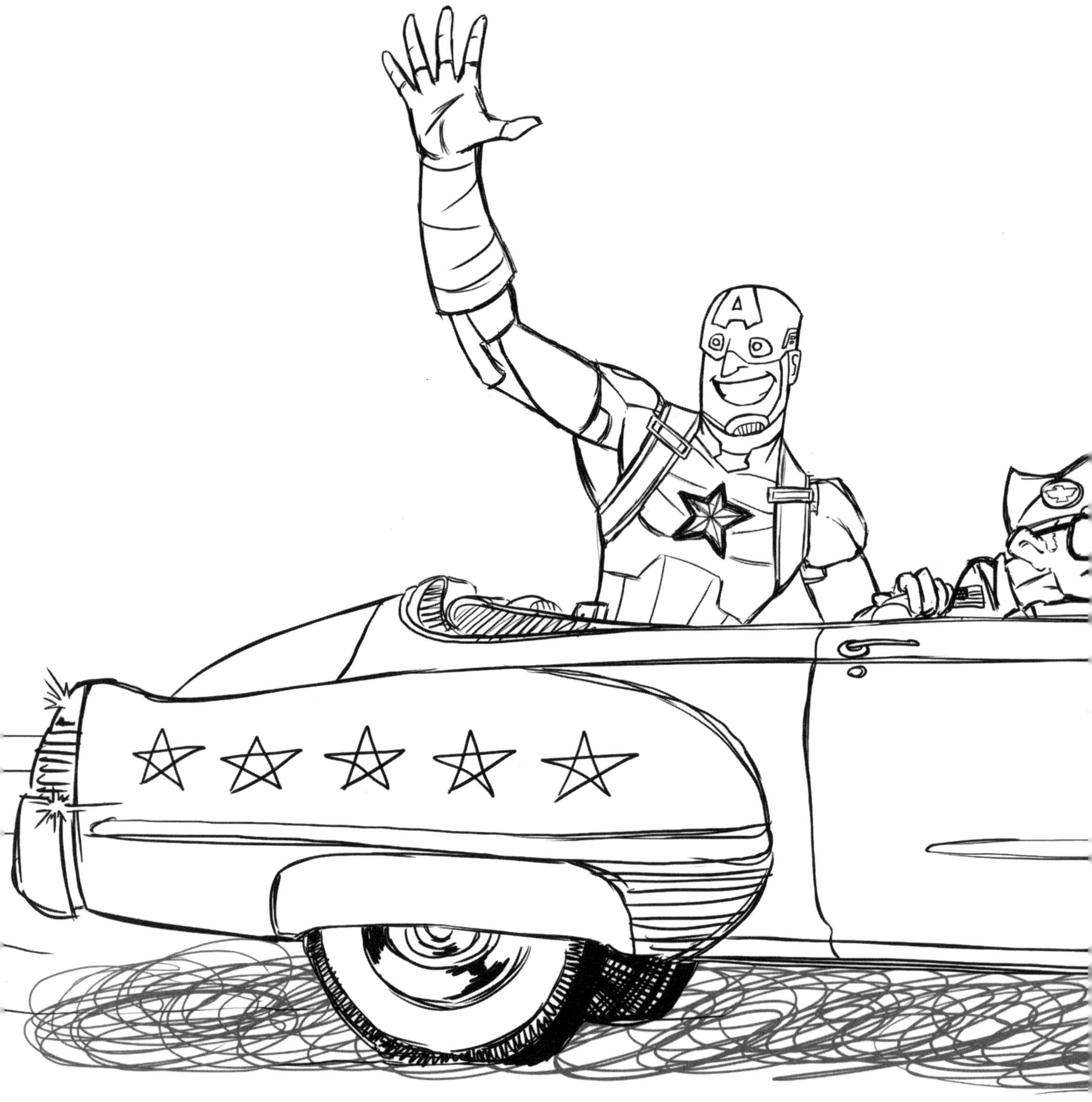

Captain America is in the Fourth of July parade!
Draw in stars and fireworks!

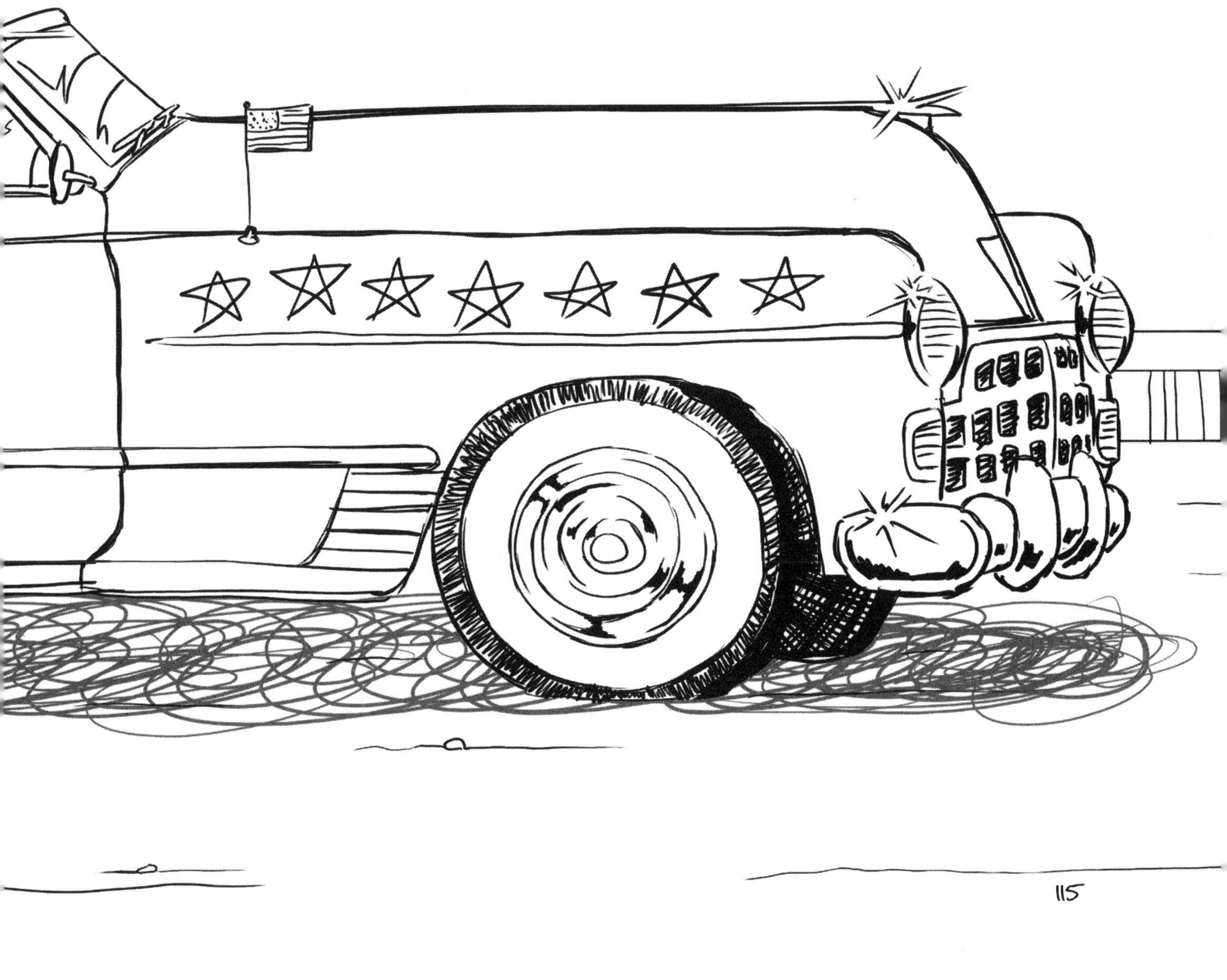

What are Spider-Man and
MJ swinging over?

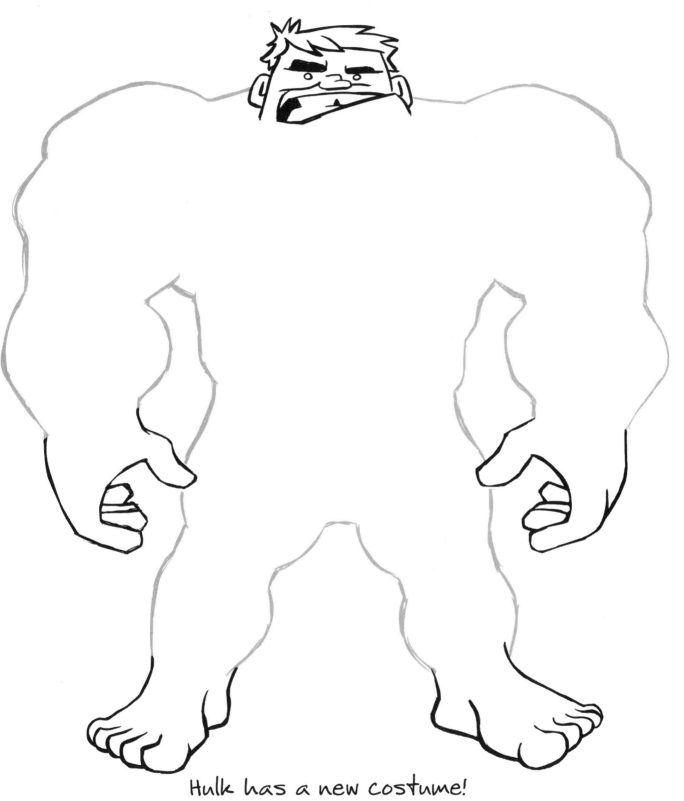

Hulk has a new costume!
Draw what it looks like!

Hulk smashed through a villain's hideout.
What's on the other side of the wall?

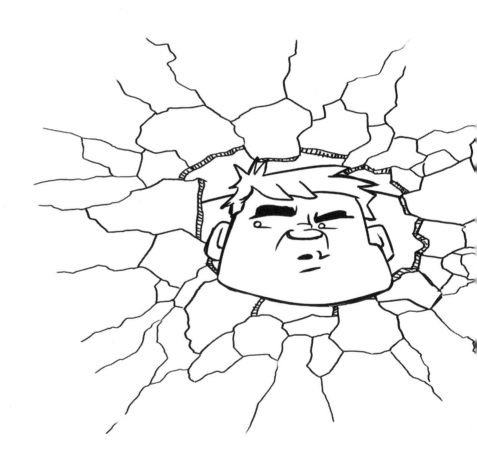

Spidey used his webs to make a statue.
What does it look like?

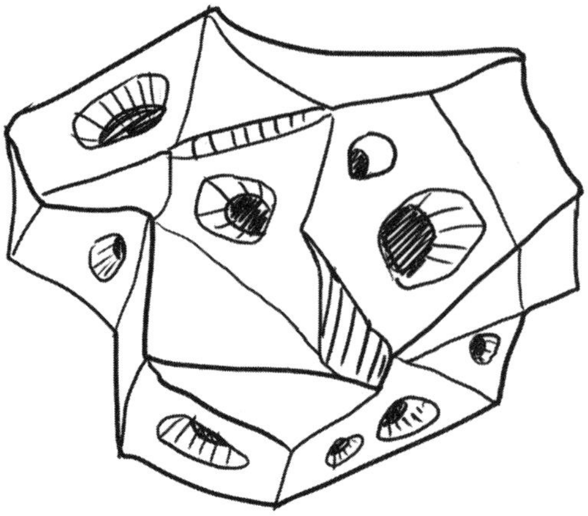

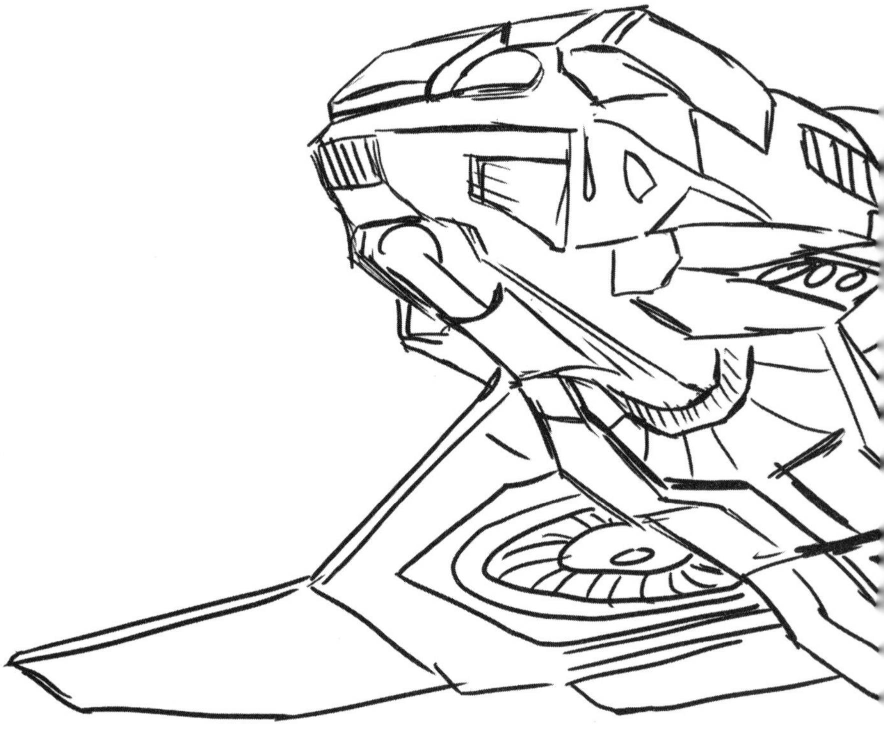

The Quinjet is in a meteor shower!
Draw the rest of the meteors!

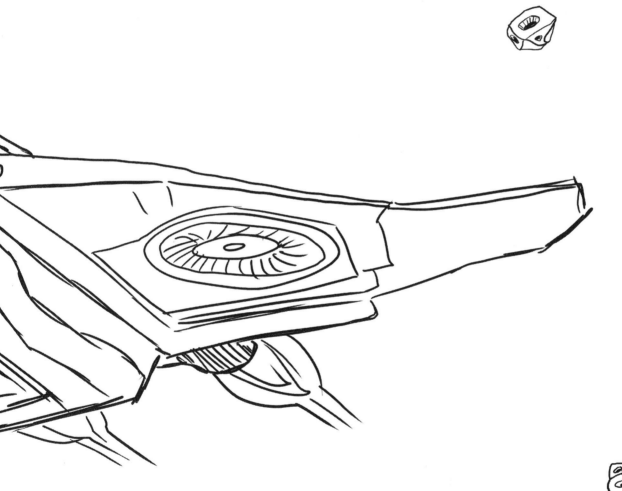

Draw the New York skyline!

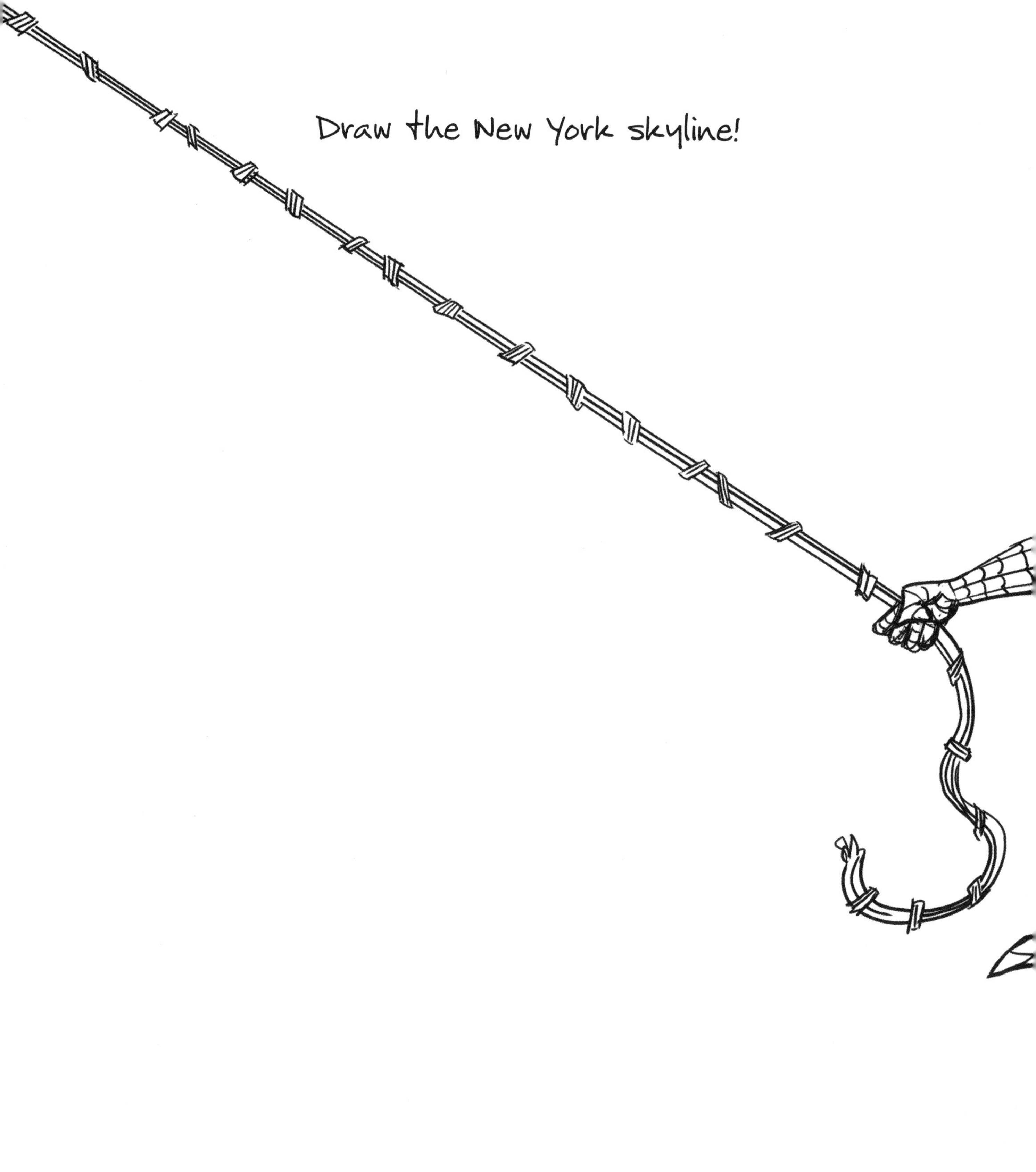

Star-Lord has new boot thrusters!
What do they look like?

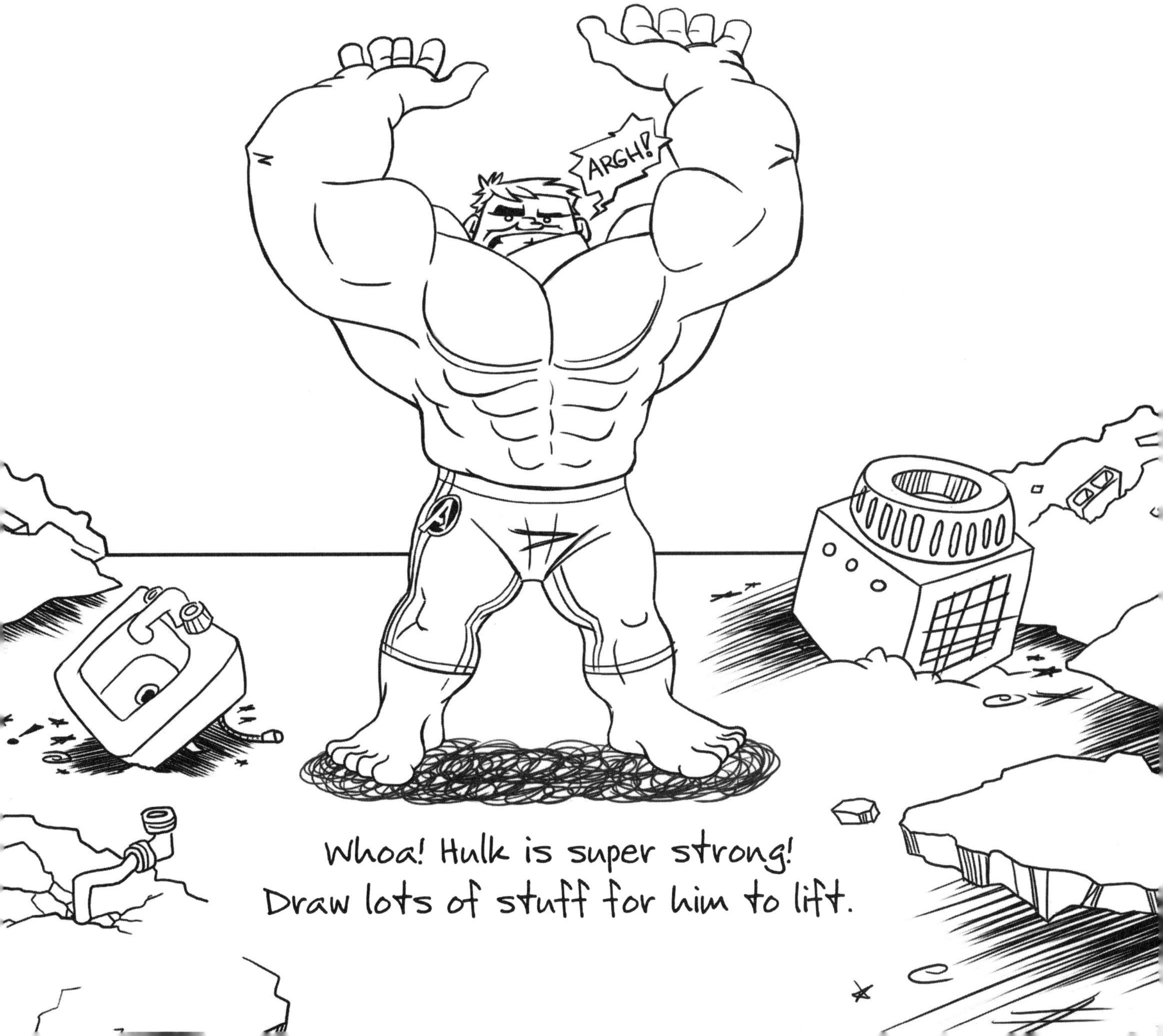
ARGH!

Whoa! Hulk is super strong!
Draw lots of stuff for him to lift.

What is the Rhino going to knock down now?

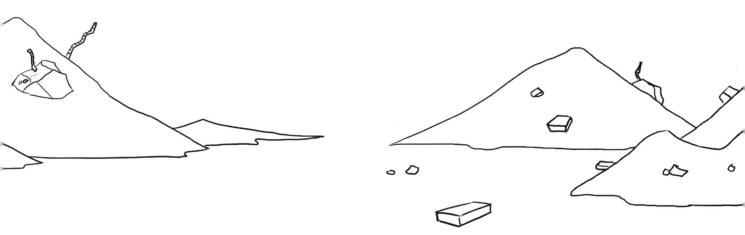

Draw YOU and a group shot of
your favorite Super Heroes!